WISHES OF HOME

THE WISHING TREE SERIES BOOK 12

BARBARA HINSKE

PRAISE FOR BARBARA HINSKE

Know an author who can grab you on the very first page so that you HAVE to keep reading? If not, then you must read Barbara Hinske. –Amazon Reviewer

Barbara Hinske writes the most engaging stories that you just cannot put down. –Amazon Reviewer

Barbara Hinske always introduces characters that become your friends and sets her novels so that you are immediately drawn in and your interest is held to the end, which is always neatly tied together, often in a surprising and unexpected way. – Amazon Reviewer

Barbara Hinske has written another warm and gentle book about people who care. The story reminds the reader that the world is full of love and compassion.... –Amazon Reviewer

You will feel uplifted and refreshed. –Amazon Reviewer

ISBN: 9781734924961
LCCN: 2022903033

Casa del Northern Publishing
Phoenix, Arizona

For our wonderful readers in My Book Friends.

ALSO BY BARBARA HINSKE

The Rosemont Series

Coming to Rosemont

Weaving the Strands

Uncovering Secrets

Drawing Close

Bringing Them Home

Shelving Doubts

Restoring What Was Lost

No Matter How Far

Novellas

The Night Train

The Christmas Club (adapted for The Hallmark Channel, 2019)

Paws and Pastries

Sweets & Treats

Novels in the Emily Series

Guiding Emily

The Unexpected Path

Over Every Hurdle (October, 2022)

Novels in the "Who's There?!" Collection

Deadly Parcel

Final Circuit

CHAPTER 1

*P*am Olson lunged for the stack of quilted placemats that a sudden gust of wind threatened to send careening across the lawn.

A thick bank of black clouds had obliterated the calm, sunny morning. The popular farmer's market held each Saturday morning on the Linden Falls square had been bustling when it opened, but shoppers were now racing to their cars, pushing strollers and pulling dogs on leashes as fast as they could go.

"I thought the storm front wasn't supposed to roll in until this evening," Irene Olson called to her daughter.

Branches of the tall trees overhead creaked and groaned.

"Let's get all this loaded back into the totes before it starts to pour." Irene began scooping up armfuls of the colorful floral tablecloths, placemats, dishcloths, and table runners she sewed and sold at the market.

Pam helped her mother in her booth most Saturday mornings and was familiar with the routine. She swung into action and the two women packed the inventory and took down the tent in record time.

"Go bring your car to the curb," Pam said as thunder rumbled. "We don't have time to ferry all of this to where you're parked. I'll start moving the totes to the curb." She pointed to a spot at the edge of the square.

Irene grabbed her satchel and the cash box and ran.

Pam stacked two large plastic totes on top of each other and sprinted to the curb where she deposited them on the sidewalk. She ran back to retrieve more totes, grateful that her day job as a personal trainer assured she was in strong physical shape.

She placed her final load with the other totes and lifted her eyes to take in the busy scene on the square as she waited for her mother. The other vendors were all breaking down their booths and closing early.

Behind them, the tallest tree on the square—the famous linden tree locals called the Wishing Tree— swayed in the wind. As the branches thrashed from side to side, Pam noted at least a dozen pieces of paper tied to the tree with string.

She smiled to herself. Folklore in Linden Falls held that the Wishing Tree was magical—if you wrote your wish on a piece of paper and tied it to the tree, it would come true. *Wishes in branches tied with string. Someone's hopes. Another's dreams.* That's what they always said.

She'd lost faith in the Wishing Tree until just recently. When she and Steve Turner had gotten together on Valentine's Day despite the no-dating vow they had each taken, her mother and Neva Cabot—the keeper of the wishes—were convinced the Wishing Tree was responsible. Pam was inclined to agree.

Irene pulled up as a car was leaving. She parallel-parked in the vacant spot with expert precision and opened the hatchback of her SUV.

Pam got busy loading totes as Irene filled the back seat. Everything had its place, and they finished the familiar task just as the wind picked up even more.

"Get in." Irene raised her voice to be heard. "I'll drop you at your car."

Pam glanced back at the Wishing Tree. As Pam watched, Neva Cabot came barreling down the steps of the Wishing Tree Inn and raced toward the Wishing Tree. As keeper of the wishes, Neva removed them from the tree before inclement weather and stored them in plastic sleeves inside binders. She'd been doing that for decades.

Pam opened the passenger door and leaned in. "Neva's headed to the tree to take down the wishes. I'm going to help her."

"That's a sweet idea, honey, but you're going to get soaked."

"It's okay. I'll see you tomorrow at lunch."

"Twelve-thirty at the Wishing Tree Inn."

Pam nodded as she shut the car door, pulled her hoodie up over her head, and ran toward the Wishing Tree.

Neva fumbled with the knot in a string holding a wish to the tree. She'd been engrossed in payroll records and hadn't noticed the darkening sky outside her window. When the first drops of rain pelted her window, she'd looked out at the tree and seen the large number of wishes twirling in the wind. She hadn't stopped for her jacket on her way out the door, and now she sorely missed the small pair of scissors that she kept tucked in a pocket for situations like this one.

"Let me get that," Pam said as she drew up to Neva.

Neva stepped back, brushing a wet hank of hair from her face. "Thank goodness."

Pam pulled her house key out of her purse and used it to saw through the string.

The rain was coming down in sheets.

"I thought I'd have to leave it and come back with scissors after I got the rest."

"I'll help you with the others." Pam stepped behind Neva and they set to the task of removing the increasingly soggy wishes from the tree.

When they'd finished, the two women dashed across the street and up the steps onto the inn's porch.

Neva turned to Pam as soon as they were under cover. "It's been years since it's rained this hard," she said, wiping away the water that dripped off her chin. She chuckled. "To tell you the truth, it was fun. I used to love to play outside in the rain when I was a kid."

"Me, too," Pam said. "It's a shame we don't let ourselves enjoy downpours that way as adults."

"I think we just did," Neva said, her eyes twinkling. "Let's take these inside," she added, holding up the wishes she'd removed from the tree, "and spread them out to dry. I'll bring us some tea and scones. We can catch up."

Pam checked her watch. "That's awfully nice, but I've got an appointment with Vera at Curl Up & Dye at two. I don't want to be late for her. You know how she gets."

"I sure do. That gives us half an hour. Just enough time for a nice visit."

The two women entered the inn and Neva led them to her private sitting room at the rear of the first floor. A long table was positioned against the wall, next to a bookcase filled with binders. Each spine was labeled with the year.

"I ran out of room in the cellar and had to make a place here for more wishes. This is where I lay them out to dry before I put them in the binders." Neva peeled a soggy paper off the top of her stack and carefully placed it on the table.

"I can do these while you make tea," Pam offered.

"Good idea." Neva handed her stack of wishes to Pam and headed for the kitchen.

Pam carefully separated the wishes and placed them on the table, taking care not to add to the damage already inflicted by the rain.

She perused the wishes. Three asked for restored health for themselves or a loved one, one person wanted a promotion at work, five longed for true love, and another asked to be admitted to a certain college.

One wish was longer than the others. Written in a child's hand, the ink was smeared and running from the rain, giving it a tearful effect. Pam bent over to read it.

I wish for a dog shelter where they don't kill dogs. My mom took me to get a dog for my birthday, but we could only get one. There were two I loved and the sign on their cages said it was their last day. That means that if no one came after us, they would put the other dog to sleep. I can't stop crying about him. I hope he got to go to his forever home. I want there to be a place in Linden Falls where all the dogs and cats can live.

Pam swallowed hard and re-read the message. The signature had almost been washed away. She picked up the paper and held it to the window. The first two letters were an "L" and an "a." She couldn't make out the rest.

Neva came into the room, carrying a tray with a teapot, pitcher of cream, sugar bowl, cups, and a plate of scones. She set the tray on a small table by the fireplace.

"What have you got there?"

Pam kept her back to the older woman, blinking hard. She took a deep breath.

Neva came up behind her and put her hand on Pam's shoulder. "You've found one of those wishes, haven't you? The kind that tears into your heart?"

Pam nodded. "I'll bet you've seen plenty of them over the years."

"I have," Neva said, taking the wish and reading it. She handed it back to Pam when she was done.

"How do you handle it?"

"If I can take some action to make the wish come true, I do it. If not, I pray for them." Neva drew Pam to one of the wing chairs by the fireplace and handed her a cup of tea and a scone.

"Is there something you can do to start a no-kill shelter in Linden Falls?" Neva asked.

"I have no idea," Pam replied. "I've never thought about it."

"Well—it's something to keep in mind." Neva settled into the chair opposite Pam and took a sip of her tea. "What have you been up to? The last time I saw you was right here—on Valentine's Day—when you were having dinner with that hunky Steve Turner."

Pam blushed at the memory. "I'm sure my mom has told you we're dating."

"She has. I'm so pleased."

"He's a wonderful guy. We're taking it slow, but so far, so good."

"There's no reason that won't continue." Neva nibbled her scone.

"And what about you?" Pam asked. "I hear that you have a suitor, too."

Neva blushed. "We are just getting to know each other again after all these years."

Pam smiled knowingly, then took a bite of her scone and moaned.

"These are Carly's latest creation. Lemon lavender poppy seed. We sell out of them every day. The rain kept people away or we wouldn't be having these now."

"They are divine," Pam said, covering her mouth with her hand as she chewed.

"How's your house?"

"As soon as I install the entry light I've ordered from Duncan's Hardware, I'll be all finished. I'd love to have you over to show you what I've done."

"That would be so much fun. Your grandmother and I went way back. I've been inside that house more times than I can count. I'm so pleased you bought it and saved it from being torn down. I'd like to see what you've done with it."

Pam grinned. "I'll have you and my mom over for dinner."

"Are you happy to be done?"

"To tell you the truth, I don't know what I'm going to do with my free time."

Neva tilted her head and looked at the young woman. "Maybe that wish will give you some ideas."

Pam shrugged. "I'm not sure." She finished her scone and set her cup on the tray. "I'd better be on my way."

"It's always nice to get your hair done—especially if you're going somewhere special. Are you seeing Steve tonight?"

"No." Pam cleared her throat before continuing. "We only go out on Friday nights."

"Ah…" Neva searched for words. "He must have something on Saturdays."

"You don't think that's kind of weird?"

"Sounds like you do. Why don't you ask him?"

Pam shook her head. "I don't want to be a nosey woman."

"You know best," Neva said, rising from her chair. "I appreciate your coming to my rescue with the wishes."

"Thank you for the tea and scones. Tell Carly they're fabulous."

Neva walked Pam to the front door and the two women hugged.

Pam stepped onto the porch. The rain had stopped, and the sun was inching its way through the clouds. She turned back to Neva. "That wish broke my heart."

Neva reached over and squeezed her arm.

"I'm not going to forget about it," Pam said as she walked down the steps and headed to her car.

CHAPTER 2

*S*teve Turner sprinted to catch up with Pam as she hurried to her car in the parking lot of Linden Falls Fitness. "Where are you off to?" he asked, glancing at the thick bank of dark clouds overhead. "It's going to start pouring any minute."

"Seems like it's done nothing but rain lately." Pam spun around, her ponytail of thick chestnut locks brushing his face as he leaned in to kiss her.

"Jed called. My entryway fixture is in."

Steve nodded sagely as fat raindrops began to pelt them. "That explains racing into a storm."

Pam cuffed his arm as she opened her car door. "I only have thirty minutes before my next client, but it's enough time to swing by Duncan's Hardware to pick it up."

"Need some help? I've got the next hour free."

"That'd be great!" She slid in behind the wheel as Steve raced around the back of the car and got in on the passenger side.

"Installing this fixture is the last thing I need to do to

finish the renovation of my grandmother's house," she said.

"You mean *your* house," Steve corrected. "She'd be so proud of what you've done for the place."

"You really think so?"

"I'm certain of it. You've got a decorator's eye, that's for sure. You're a terrific personal trainer—all your clients love you—but you could make a living in the interior design business."

Pam hit the lever to increase the windshield wiper speed to high. Rain came down in sheets. "I'm anxious to be done, but I'm a little bit sad, too."

"I get that. You've been working on your house every free moment for the past year."

"Not every free moment." She glanced at him and blushed. "Someone's been distracting me—ever since Valentine's Day."

"I hope they've been welcome distractions?"

"You know they have been."

He reached across and rubbed her knee.

"You've also helped me with a bunch of projects that would have taken me much longer on my own." She squeezed his hand. "I really am grateful."

Steve shrugged. "I could reach a lot of stuff that you would have needed a ladder for."

"Being big, strong, and six foot four is a natural advantage. I'll give you that," she said.

"I provided brawn—you were the brains. All the design ideas came from you."

"We made a great team," Pam said, entering the parking lot behind Duncan's. "I don't know what I'm going to do with myself when I'm all done."

"I've got some ideas." Steve cupped her chin with his hand and kissed her.

"I'd like that," she murmured as she pulled away. "But right now, we need to get that fixture so I can be back at the gym in time for my next client."

PAM SMILED at Jed as she waited for him to finish helping Calvin, their town reporter, who had a million questions about how to replace a bathroom faucet. When Courtney —Calvin's new girlfriend and Linden Fall's recent heroine —joined them, Calvin immediately acted like he knew all there was to know about plumbing and Courtney began telling Jed of other updates they were planning in Calvin's home.

Jed looked past them and caught Pam's eye, motioning with his head toward the back of the store where they kept special orders. Pam knew the area well. She and Steve began weaving their way through the aisles of hardware and past the paint section. They were walking down a row of tile when a familiar voice called to Steve.

He turned to find a well-proportioned blonde wearing too-tight designer workout wear waving at him.

"Steve," Susan Wilbanks called in the sultry purr that she reserved for any man in her vicinity. "What are *you* doing *here* in the middle of the afternoon? I didn't know you played hooky during the workday." She raised an eyebrow coyly. It seemed that having everything she'd ever wanted, including an obnoxious Range Rover, the biggest house in Linden Falls, and a new anniversary diamond wasn't enough to keep her happy. Susan and her husband had separated while she focused on 'finding herself.'

"I'm helping my girlfriend pick something up," he said, as Pam joined them.

Susan's sugary expression soured. "Oh? I didn't know the two of you were an item."

"It's no secret," Steve said, placing his arm around Pam's waist. "I guess the gym isn't as much of a gossip mill as I thought."

"Hello, Susan," Pam said. "We're picking up a light fixture. What are you looking for?"

"I'm here with a friend—helping her pick out tile."

A woman in her early forties came around the end cap and joined them.

Susan waggled her fingers along the aisle and spoke to her friend. "I told you Duncan's won't have what you want. We'll need to go to one of the specialty retailers in Boston to find anything decent. I got everything out of town when we redid our house."

"I don't agree." Pam squared her shoulders. She'd remodeled her entire house—her grandmother's old house—and had purchased everything she'd needed right there in Linden Falls. At Duncan's Hardware. They'd been fair on all their prices, prompt with all her special orders, and more than generous with their advice and expertise. She wasn't going to let the snooty Susan Wilbanks say anything derogatory about her favorite retailer.

"You're her, aren't you?" Susan's friend asked, bringing a hand to her heart.

"What're you talking about?" Susan almost spat the words.

"The woman on social media. The one who's remodeled one of the old homes right here in Linden Falls?" She pushed her hair off her face. "I've watched all your videos —a bunch of them multiple times. In fact, watching you encouraged me to redo my kitchen. You have such beautiful taste."

"Gosh, thank you," Pam said. "I had no idea anyone was watching them—other than my mother and Neva."

"Duncan's shares all of them. That's where I first found you." The woman bit her lip. "I'm here to pick out backsplash tile. Susan says Duncan's doesn't have anything worthwhile, but I remember you saying that you got everything here."

"That's right."

"Could I just ask you a quick question about a couple of tiles I'm thinking about? Do you have time?"

Susan's eyebrows knitted together as she narrowed her eyes.

"Give me the pickup slip and I'll get your light fixture while you help… your follower," Steve interjected.

Pam handed him the paper. She could tell he was working hard to repress a smile.

"I've only got about five minutes," Pam said, "but I'd love to see what you're considering."

The woman tapped at her phone. "This is what my cabinets and countertops look like…"

Pam took the phone and examined the screen as she and the woman walked to a display of tile on the wall.

No one noticed Susan release a huffy breath and stalk away in the other direction.

JED CAUGHT up with Pam as she was putting the seats down in the back of her SUV so Steve could load the large cardboard box containing the light fixture into her car. "Let me give you a hand with that," he said to Steve, grabbing one side of the box.

The two men lifted it into place.

"Once we install this, my house is done." Pam closed the hatchback.

"You must be excited," Jed said.

"I am."

"What's your next project?" Jed asked. "You've become one of our favorite customers."

Pam smiled at him ruefully. "I can't afford to tackle anything else right now. I need to get my tax refund first." She watched his expression fall. "Not that I'm complaining about your prices," she added quickly. "You've been more than fair to me. I'm not a contractor and I know you still gave me a big discount. I'm grateful for that."

"We were happy to do it. You gave us a ton of good publicity by tagging us in your social media posts. We got traffic on our website from those."

Pam rolled her eyes dismissively. "I can't imagine they did you much good, but I'm glad if they helped at all."

"They were awesome. You've become an influencer."

"Seriously?" She began shaking her head. "I can't imagine…"

"Listen to the man," Steve broke in. "I've seen your stories or reels or whatever they are. They're very informative and engaging. You're a natural in front of the camera."

"Exactly." Jed picked up the thread of conversation.

"Actually, you both are. That interview you did for the local TV station about the Christmas Toy Drive was fabulous. People talked about the two of you for weeks."

Pam guffawed. "You mean my mom talked about us for weeks."

"And mine," Steve added.

"Joke all you like," Jed said, "but both of you have the 'it' factor."

"Thank you, Jed." Pam patted his arm and opened her car door. "Steve and I had better get back to the gym. Our day jobs are still as personal trainers and not TV stars."

Jed rubbed his chin as he watched her car pull out of the lot. "You just never know..." he muttered under his breath.

CHAPTER 3

Steve stepped down one rung on the ladder and turned his head over his shoulder. "Okay—now try it."

He looked at the entryway light fixture hanging over his head as the bulbs sprang to life. "That's it," he called. "Come see."

Pam was at the bottom of the ladder before he stepped off it onto the floor. "It's beautiful. Exactly what I wanted." She walked down the steps to her front porch and viewed the fixture from the walkway. "It makes such a statement!"

He joined her, nodding his agreement. "I like it a lot."

"Thank you for getting up early to help me hang it," she said, wrapping her arms around his waist and pulling him to her for a kiss.

He held her close and kissed her again.

She put her hands against his chest and looked up at him. "You always play golf on Sunday. Don't you have a tee time in a few minutes?"

He brought one arm up behind her back and turned

his wrist so he could look at his watch. "I can be ten minutes late."

"I don't think so, mister. This is your first round since the course reopened this spring, and you've been talking about it for weeks." She wriggled out of his embrace. "I'm not going to get between you and golf. Have a good time and I'll see you back here for dinner."

"You don't have to cook. Why don't I take us out?"

"I *want* to cook for us. Now that my remodel is officially done, I want to celebrate with a meal in my own home."

"You deserve to celebrate. You've done an amazing job. What time?"

"Does seven work?"

"Perfect." He kissed the tip of her nose.

"Go have fun," she said as she skipped up the steps and into her house.

STEVE LUMBERED up Pam's front steps, holding two large black plastic pots containing oversized shrubs away from his starched white shirt. He set one on either side of the door and rang the bell.

Pam answered, wearing a pink-flowered wrap dress that flowed gracefully to her ankles. Her hair hung loose around her shoulders in a rare escape from her habitual ponytail.

"Wow," he said, sweeping his eyes over her as she came out onto the porch. "You're beautiful."

"You look pretty fabulous yourself," she said. "It's a

good thing Susan Wilbanks can't see you in a dress shirt and slacks. She wouldn't be able to contain herself."

"Don't even mention that woman! She's after every man in town under seventy. I feel sorry for her poor husband."

"Haven't you heard the gossip at the gym?"

He shook his head.

"Rumor has it she's getting a divorce." She ran her hands down his arms. "I'm serious. She'll be after you more than ever now."

"I'll be extra careful to avoid her," he said. "Enough about the odious Susan. I brought you these." He pointed to the potted shrubs. "To celebrate the completion of your remodel."

"Hydrangeas!" she squealed. "You remembered!" She bent to look at the plant tags stuck in each pot.

"You wanted pink ones, right?"

"Yes."

"That's what they said these are. They may take a couple of years to get established, but they should last for decades."

Pam flung her arms around him. "I want them on each side of the walkway, at the base of the steps."

Steve nodded. "That's why I got two of them."

"You are the most thoughtful man on earth."

"We can plant them next Sunday morning."

"That works. I'll water them in their pots this week." She took his hand and led him into the house. "Are you hungry?"

"Starving. I got to the course too late to grab lunch."

"Oh, no! I'm sorry. That's my fault—I kept you here too long, putting up my light." She took him to the kitchen island and pressed him onto a stool. "I've got bacon-wrapped dates, and they're ready right now." She pulled the pan out of the oven and plated the appetizer, setting it in front of him. "What would you like to drink?"

"I'd really like water," he said. "After being outside all afternoon, I'm thirsty."

She put ice in a tall glass and filled it from a pitcher in her refrigerator.

"These are delicious," he said, popping a whole, gooey date into his mouth. "You'd better get over here before I eat them all myself."

"You'll want to save room. We're having an herbed beef tenderloin with garlic mashed potatoes and roasted broccolini. Comfort food."

He rubbed his hands together.

"Were you expecting a salad for the main course?"

"That's what you usually make," he stammered. "And it's always delicious," he hastened to add.

Pam laughed. "This is a departure from my usual menu. I thought something special was in order, and the occasional serving of red meat won't hurt us."

"I wouldn't argue with that."

She opened the oven door and pulled out the roast, its caramelized crust crackling and spitting as she set it on the counter. She turned down the oven temperature and inserted a pan of trimmed broccolini misted with olive oil and dusted with sea salt and freshly ground black pepper.

Leopold appeared from nowhere and paced at the base of the cabinet, positioning himself to leap onto the counter.

"Nope," she said to her cat as she scooped him up.

"None of this is for you. I think it's time you went to the bedroom."

Steve rose from his stool and leaned toward the roast, as if pulled by an invisible thread.

She walked by him, carrying the feline who was meowing in protest.

"That looks—and smells—amazing," Steve said.

Pam grinned. "If you were a dog, your tail would be wagging a mile a minute. The roast should rest for twenty minutes before I carve it. All I have to do is mash the potatoes." She motioned for him to sit back down. "I'll be right back. How was your afternoon?" she called as she deposited Leopold in her bedroom and shut the door.

"The course was in fine shape. My game, however, was not. I need to spend some serious time at the driving range…"

Pam finished the potatoes while they chatted. She carved the roast, and they loaded up their plates.

Steve headed for her kitchen table, but Pam motioned for him to follow her. "I thought we'd eat in the dining room. It'll be my first meal in this room since," her voice caught in her throat, "since I've owned the house."

Steve put his plate on the polished walnut table and took hers from her hands, setting it next to his. He gathered Pam into his arms. "Remembering your grandmother?"

She nodded, her head against his chest.

"I'll bet this room holds a lot of wonderful memories for you." He looked down at her. "And now you get to make more memories here."

She brushed her hair off her face. "I feel all of them—my grandparents and my dad—so strongly here. We celebrated every holiday, every birthday, every milestone, and countless ordinary moments in between, in this room—at this very table." She cast her eyes around the room until they settled on their plates. "And our food is getting cold. Let's eat."

They sat down and Steve listened as she recounted details from happy childhood gatherings in her house. When they were done, they took their plates into the kitchen.

"I thought we could have dessert and coffee by my fire pit. Would you mind lighting the flame while I dish up the dessert?"

"Great idea. What're we having?"

She shook her head, a Cheshire Cat grin on her face. "You'll just have to wait and see."

Steve got the fire going and pulled a cushioned love seat close to it. He found a woven throw in a storage bench and draped it across the back of the love seat.

Pam joined him, carrying a tray with a coffee carafe, pottery mugs, and two plates with slices of fragrant pound cake dusted with powdered sugar.

"What's that?" Steve asked.

"It's my grandmother's sherry cake. It's an old family recipe."

"It smells amazing."

"Mace gives it that fabulous aroma."

"I've never even heard of mace before, but I'm a fan now."

Pam handed him a plate and a mug of coffee before settling herself next to him on the loveseat.

"You've done a remarkable job with this house. You've preserved the historical character while making it functional and comfortable by today's standards. I'm going to sound like a broken record, but you've got an instinctive talent for home design."

She finished her cake and put her plate down, settling against him. "Thank you. I've always loved decorating, but this project has shown me I love design and remodeling, too. I've made plenty of mistakes on this place," she pointed to a gutter that hung askew, "but I learned something with every project and I got better with each one. The folks at Duncan's answered all my questions and were there for me every step of the way—I couldn't have done this without them. And your help these past few months has been invaluable."

"I didn't do much—only provided a bit of muscle now and again."

"You did more than that." She shivered and burrowed into him with a heavy sigh.

Steve draped the throw around her shoulders.

"That sounded like an unhappy sigh."

"I'm a little sad," she replied. "I don't have any reason to go into Duncan's anymore—except to get parts for the occasional repair. I'll miss looking at new trends in tile, like I did with that woman today." She shifted her weight to look at him. "Did you know that new colors and designs have hit in the few months since I bought the tile for this place?" She sighed again. "But there's no point in window shopping."

"Can't you keep yourself current with those board things of yours that you were always looking at on your phone?"

"Pinterest? What's the use? This place is done." She

pulled back to look at him. "To be honest, I'm thinking about a wish I pulled off the Wishing Tree."

It was Steve's turn to look quizzical. "I thought they were supposed to stay on the tree."

"They are—unless it's going to rain. Neva takes them off the tree and stores them in binders so they don't get ruined."

"She must have hundreds of them."

"More like thousands." Pam sunk against the cushions. "I saw her frantically trying to take some down before a storm hit, so I helped her. We took them to the inn and spread them out to dry. I read a few. One of them really got to me." She recited the wish to him, almost verbatim.

Steve swallowed hard before replying. "I can see why. That's a real tearjerker."

"Right? I wish I could do something to help this kid. I can't seem to forget it."

Steve pulled her close to him and began trailing kisses along the side of her face and her neck. "I can try to take your mind off things…"

CHAPTER 4

*S*teve stood and brushed dirt from his jeans.

Pam trained the hose on the second hydrangea bush he had planted for her. "Thanks for these. They're going to be beautiful. This makes two Sunday mornings in a row. I promise I won't make a habit of asking you to come over before your golf game to help me."

He sat on the step and picked up his mug of coffee. "I don't mind at all. Ask me anytime. What are you doing today?"

"I'm meeting Mom at the Wishing Tree Inn for a late lunch. When's your tee time?"

"I'm not playing golf today, actually. I'm taking my sister Carol's kids to a movie so she and Tom can have time to themselves. After that, I'm going to pick up dinner to take back for all of us. The hospital ER is short-staffed and Tom's been working double shifts. This is his first Sunday off in months."

"That's really nice of you."

"I love my niece and nephews. It'll be fun."

Pam stowed the hose and joined him on the step. "Why don't you swing by here after the movie? I'll make a lasagna and a big salad. And I've got chocolate chip cookies I can pull out of the freezer. You can take it all to your sister's."

"Now who's being nice? Do you have time for all that?"

Pam nodded. "Like we talked about, I have nothing but time on my hands now that I'm done with the house."

"All right—but on one condition."

She raised an eyebrow.

"You come with us for dinner. I'd like you to get to know the whole family." He grasped her hand and brought it to his lips. "I think it's about time."

Pam felt herself flush. "Are you sure your sister won't mind?"

"She's been after me for weeks to bring you over."

"Then—yes—that sounds like fun." She stood. "I'd better get busy. I can run to the grocery before I meet Mom."

Steve circled his arms around her waist and brought her to him. "I was thinking about your mom this morning. Does she have any remodeling projects you can do at her house?"

"I've been asking her that for weeks. She says she's happy with her house the way it is."

Steve laughed. "My parents say the same thing. They've got everything the way they want it and can't see the point in changing anything. Still, it wouldn't hurt to ask Irene again. Maybe she'll change her mind and you'll be doing what you love again."

"I guess." She stood on her tiptoes and kissed him. "See you after the movie."

"I'll text when we're on our way to pick you up."

"I THOUGHT I saw the two of you come in." Neva leaned down to hug first Irene and then Pam. "Janie and Carly aren't here today and we're short-staffed or I would have come over earlier. This table has the best view of the Wishing Tree on the square, but it's tucked away in the corner and easily forgotten." She touched the china pot that sat in the middle of the table. "This is stone cold!" She clicked her tongue. "Sorry about that. I'll get Breeze to bring you a new pot."

"Thank you," Irene said. "We're in the middle of a big discussion. Pam's trying to convince me to tear up my completely functional house so she can remodel it."

Neva chuckled. "I know you, Irene. You're not one for change."

"My place may not be done up in today's style, but I love my flowery drapes and thick carpet. I don't want anything different."

Neva rested the teapot on her hip. "Not even that bathroom of yours that you keep complaining about?" She winked at Pam. "You just told me last week that you'd like to get rid of the tub and put in a walk-in shower."

"That's brilliant!" Pam seized on the idea. "Your master bath could use a complete makeover. Nothing's been done in it since before I was born." She looked pointedly at her mother.

"That's true… but I'm not sure I want to spend the money…"

"You won't have to spend a dime," Pam cut her off. "I can easily do most of the work myself and I know who to hire for the things I can't do. I'll pay for the materials—I'm getting a tax refund that should cover the expense. It'll be your birthday present!"

"Now that's an offer you can't refuse," Neva said before moving in the direction of the kitchen.

"She's right. You can't refuse, Mom. You know you'd love an updated bathroom and… well… I need another project."

Irene cocked her head to one side and regarded her daughter. "You're feeling a bit adrift after finishing your house, aren't you?"

"I think I am. Sounds crazy, right?"

"Not really. It's natural to feel that when you complete a big task." She inhaled slowly. "I don't want this project to be a drain on you. You work too hard as it is."

"It won't be, Mom. I'll enjoy the work and I'd love to do this for you." She scrunched up her nose. "I hate thinking of you in that bathroom with the stained grout and Formica countertops. You deserve something nicer than that."

Breeze swept by the table, depositing the steaming hot pot in the center.

Irene pursed her lips as she poured them each a fresh cup of the fragrant liquid. "I'm not sure what I even want. I don't like all this modern stuff I see on TV."

"We'll make sure it goes with the rest of your house. There'll be plenty of tiles and fixtures to choose from. Let's go to Duncan's next weekend to see what's available.

You can bring brochures and samples home to think about what you'd like."

"It seems like such a daunting process."

Pam reached across the table and took her mother's hand. "It won't be. I promise you this will be fun. I'll be with you every step of the way. We won't select anything until you're sure."

Irene squeezed her daughter's hand. A smile played at her lips. "If you're sure?"

"Positive! I'd suggest we walk across the square to Duncan's right now, but I have to get home to make dinner for Steve's sister's family."

Irene's smile broke free. "You're having his sister over for dinner?"

Pam shook her head. "I'm making lasagna and a salad to take to their house." She filled her mother in on the recently concocted plan.

"That sounds lovely, dear." She took a sip of her tea. "Do you want to take them a loaf of my sourdough bread to go with it?"

"That would be terrific. I meant to buy a baguette for garlic bread at the grocery this morning, but I forgot." Pam drained the remaining tea from her cup.

"I just baked two loaves this morning." Irene caught Neva's eye on the other side of the dining room and signaled for the check. "You can stop by my house to pick up the bread on your way home."

"That'd be great. It's after two already so I need to get back to my kitchen. I'm not sure when the movie lets out, but I'm assuming they'll pick me up between five and five-thirty."

"Gosh, you'd better get moving!"

"I put the lasagna together before I came here, but I still have to make the salad."

"That's my organized daughter," Irene said with an unmistakable note of pride in her voice.

Neva brought them the check. "Do I sense that you've come to an agreement on remodeling that bathroom of yours?"

"You are positively psychic, Neva," Irene said. "Pam's talked me into it."

Neva's eyes sparkled.

"And—to tell you the truth—I'm really looking forward to it."

CHAPTER 5

"That smells great, Ms. Olson!" Riley called from the back seat of Steve's SUV.

"Pam, please," she replied. "Thank you. I hope all of you like lasagna?" She shifted in her seat so she could look at the three children behind her.

Ben—age twelve, Riley—age ten, and Emma—age eight, were all nodding. "I've got a big green salad, home-made bread that my mom baked this morning, and chocolate chip cookies, too."

"Sweet," Ben said when she mentioned the cookies. "Those are my favorites."

"Are you going to marry Uncle Steve?" Emma blurted out.

Pam rocked back in her seat.

"Pam and I are dating." Steve lifted his gaze to the rear view mirror and made eye contact with Emma. "We're very good friends."

Emma's brows knitted together. "Mom says the two of

you should get married. If you do—if you have a fancy wedding—I want to be part of it."

"Duly noted," Steve said, turning to Pam and mouthing the word "sorry."

Pam rolled her eyes and smiled. "What's your favorite cookie, Emma?" she asked, changing the subject.

Steve's niece and nephews debated the merits of chocolate chip, snickerdoodle, and oatmeal raisin until Steve turned into the driveway of an imposing, two-story brick home on a generous lot surrounded by mature trees.

"This is lovely," Pam said as she leaned forward to unbuckle her seat belt and peered out the windshield.

"I figured you'd like it," Steve said. "Wait until you see the inside. They've done a great job with it."

The front door opened and a tall, slender woman bearing a striking resemblance to Steve raced down the steps.

The kids sprang out of the car and ran toward her.

"How was the movie?" she asked as Ben and Riley continued past her to the house. Emma flung her arms around her mother's waist and Carol hugged her.

"I loved it! Ben and Riley said it was babyish and that they're too old for Disney movies."

Pam and Steve joined his sister and niece. "Don't you believe them," Steve said. "I could tell that they liked it as much as you did."

"You're never too old for a Disney movie," Pam said. "I still watch my favorites."

"Really?" Emma regarded Pam thoughtfully.

"Absolutely. *Little Mermaid*, *Beauty and the Beast*, and *Cinderella* are my favorites."

"I like those, but *Frozen* is mine."

"Maybe we can have you over for a girl's movie night and binge watch them," Carol said, extending her hand to Pam. "Hi, I'm Carol."

"Sorry—I should have made the introduction," Steve said.

"No worries." Pam shook Carol's hand.

"I've heard so much about you. I feel like I already know you," Carol said.

"Same here," Pam said, flushing with pleasure at the revelation that Steve had been talking to his family about her.

Tom came around the side of the house, chasing a golden retriever.

"Sugar!" Emma dropped to her knees and threw her arms wide. The elderly dog trotted into her embrace.

"Take her around back, Emma," her father said, pointing in the direction that he had come from, "and make sure the gate gets closed."

"Okay, Daddy." Emma slipped her hand under the dog's collar and they walked toward the gate to the backyard.

"You must be Pam," Tom said, introducing himself. "We're so glad you could join us."

"And thank you so much for making dinner. You didn't have to do that. We should have cooked…"

Pam touched Carol's elbow to stop her. "Nonsense. I love to cook—this was fun for me. I rarely make lasagna just for myself."

"Speaking of…" Steve broke in. "I spent the drive over here smelling it. I can't wait to eat. I'm starved." He moved to his SUV and opened the hatchback.

Tom followed him.

"The table's all set," Carol said. "Do you need help?"

"We've got this," Tom said.

"Come on, Pam. Let me get you something to drink. I'll call the kids to wash their hands and we'll be ready to sit down."

Pam followed Carol up the steps and into the house. Steve was right. Carol and Tom had infused their home with casual elegance. Comfortable and welcoming, the furnishings invited you to pull up a chair and relax. The couple had achieved the look she admired and hoped she'd emulated in her own house.

"I love what you've done with your home," she said to Carol as they placed the food on the kitchen island.

"Thank you," Carol said. "We had the help of a decorator. She gave us exactly what we wanted. I love home decor and watch all the shows on HGTV, but I don't have the interior design skills that Steve tells me you have."

Pam felt herself flush with pride again.

Carol opened a drawer and retrieved salad tongs and a serrated spatula. She inserted the spatula into the lasagna, cutting through the gooey, melted cheese on top. "This looks amazing," she said, cutting out the first piece and moving it deftly to a plate.

"I'd love to see your place," Carol said. "If you don't mind me inviting myself over." She grinned sheepishly.

"I'd be happy to show you. Maybe you can all come for dinner one night."

"On one condition," Carol said, removing three bottles of salad dressing from the refrigerator and placing them next to the salad. "You let us bring in the food."

Pam laughed. "You don't need to do that."

Carol swept her arm over the spread on the kitchen island. "After all of this, I'd like to."

"All right," Pam said. "It's a deal."

Carol stepped to the doorway of the kitchen. "Okay everybody. Dinner's ready."

The kitchen quickly buzzed with activity as Steve, Tom, and the kids filled their plates and took them to the dining room table.

Pam and Carol were the last to enter the dining room. Steve had saved a seat for Pam next to him.

"Ben—go sit with your uncle," Carol directed. She looked at her brother. "You see her every day. I want to be next to Pam so we can talk."

Steve nodded his approval as Ben did as he was told.

Pam and Carol spent the meal engrossed in conversation about home decor trends and their favorite HGTV shows.

Steve, Tom, and the boys served themselves second helpings of everything. When everyone was done, Ben and Riley cleared the table.

"Can I bring the cookies to the table?" Emma asked.

"That'd be very nice, sweetie," Carol said.

Emma returned with the plate of cookies and passed it around the table.

"One at a time," Tom said as Ben began stacking them in his hand.

Ben looked to his mother in appeal.

"You've already touched them, so you can keep them. You shouldn't take more than you can eat."

"I'm gonna eat all of these," Ben assured her, shoving a cookie in his mouth.

Pam caught Ben's eye and winked at him.

Ben gave her the thumbs-up sign with both hands.

Conversation lulled as everyone helped themselves and enjoyed the sweet treats.

Pam leaned toward the kids. "I'm wondering if any of you kids know something."

Ben, Riley, and Emma all looked at her.

"Someone, actually." Pam cleared her throat. "Do you know a kid who recently adopted a dog from an animal shelter? As a birthday present?"

Three sets of eyes stared back at her. All three children shook their heads "no."

Pam pursed her lips. "Do any of you have a friend whose name begins with the letters L-a?"

Ben and Emma again shook their heads "no."

"There's a kid in my math section named Larry," Ben said.

Pam sat up straighter. "Does he have a dog?"

Ben shrugged. "I don't know him very well." He looked at Pam. "I could ask him."

"Would you? I'd like to know."

"Why?" Ben asked.

Steve raised an eyebrow at Pam and turned to his nephew. "I think Pam has a very good reason, but I don't think we should talk about it right now."

"Okay," Ben said.

"I don't want you to do anything you don't want to do." Pam said, glancing at Carol.

"It's up to you, Ben," Carol said.

"It's fine. We're in the same class. I can find out for you."

"Thank you," Pam said. "It's a long story, for another time."

Tom stood. "Speaking of the time, I think you kids need to finish your homework."

"Pam and I both have clients when the gym opens at five-thirty tomorrow morning. We'd better get going."

Carol and Tom walked Pam and Steve to the car.

"I can't wait to see you again," Carol said, giving Pam a hug.

"Thank you for bringing dinner," Tom said. "It was delicious." He shook Steve's hand. "And thank *you* for taking the kids off of our hands for the afternoon."

"My pleasure," Steve said. "I love spending time with them."

Carol and Tom slid their arms around each other's waist and watched as Steve's car drove away.

PAM TURNED to Steve as soon as they were out of the driveway. "Do you mind that I asked Ben to find out if this Larry got a rescue dog for his birthday?"

Steve shook his head. "That's innocent enough." He reached across the console and took her hand. "You're still thinking about that wish, aren't you?"

"I can't get it out of my head." She took in a deep breath and let it out in a rush. "I don't know why. It's not like there's anything I can do about it."

"What will you do if Ben's classmate got a rescue for his birthday? It doesn't mean that he wrote that wish and tied it to the tree."

"I know. Honestly, I'm not sure why I'm so focused on this." She bit her lower lip. "I feel compelled to find out."

"Do you have a gut feeling that you can't ignore?"

"Exactly!"

"Then don't ignore it. There's a subconscious reason you're drawn to the person who wrote the wish."

"You really believe that?"

"Yep." He glanced at her. "I'd do the same thing."

Pam squeezed his hand. "I feel so much better."

They continued the short drive to her house in companionable silence. Steve parked at the curb and walked her to her door.

"Thank you for making that wonderful dinner for my family," Steve said. "And be sure to thank Irene for the bread. It was really nice of her to contribute it." He put his arm around Pam's waist as they climbed the steps to her front door.

"Will do. I enjoyed meeting your sister and her family. They're great."

"You liked them, then?"

"Very much."

"They all loved you. I'm sure my sister will call me later to tell me not to screw this up." He turned Pam to face him.

Pam laughed. "Your sister adores you. Anybody can see that."

Steve pulled her close.

"I'd invite you in, but we both have very early starts tomorrow."

Steve leaned in and kissed her.

Pam slid her arms around his neck and pressed against him as their kiss grew in intensity. She finally pulled back.

"Kissing me like that is not the way to get rid of me, you know," Steve whispered in her ear.

She rested her forehead on his chest.

"But I know you're right. Is Wednesday still your early day? My last client is done at four. Maybe we could go for a run and then grab dinner? It's supposed to be a beautiful day."

"My Tuesday client had to reschedule to Wednesday this week. Tuesday will be my early day."

"I'm working until eight on Tuesday."

"Mom wants to meet at the Crooked Porch Café for coffee on Tuesday afternoon, anyway," Pam said. "She's got inspiration photos to show me. Now that I've talked her into letting me redo her bathroom, she's hot to trot."

"That's nice—for both of you."

"It is. She's had so much fun scrolling through Pinterest and looking at home decor magazines. It'll put a spring in her step."

"You may have started something. After the bathroom's done, she may want to redo the rest of the house."

Pam grinned. "I doubt that, but it would be fine with me if she did."

"I'll just have to content myself with seeing you at the gym this week. How about dinner on Friday night?"

"That works," Pam said. "I'm free either Friday or Saturday."

"Friday it is," Steve said, pulling her back to him for another kiss.

Pam unlocked her door and stepped inside, turning to wave at him as he started his car and pulled away.

What was it about Steve Turner and Saturday nights?

Leopold meowed loudly as she deposited her purse on

the entryway table. She scooped up her cat and hugged him to her, burying her face in his fur.

"I'm not going to worry about it," she murmured. "We're just dating, and I don't need to know."

She turned out the porch light and headed for bed.

CHAPTER 6

*P*am walked into the Crooked Porch Café at quarter past three. The dining room was almost empty.

Irene held up a hand to wave at her daughter as she came in.

Pam spotted her mother at a large booth in the back. The table in front of her was littered with papers and a stack of magazines stood at one end.

Her mother had, indeed, been busy. Pam couldn't remember when she'd last seen her so happy and excited.

Irene scooted over on the bench as Pam walked up to the booth. "Here," she said, patting the seat next to her. "Sit with me on my side, so it's easier to go over all this."

Pam sank down next to her mother.

"You weren't kidding when you said you had a lot to show me." Pam reached over and hugged Irene.

"I don't know where to start." Irene bit her lip.

"Do you have any pictures of entire bathrooms that you like?"

Irene nodded.

Pam leaned across the table. "Some of these are just close-ups of tile and fixtures." She tapped a photo of an elaborately tiled shower. "Let's start with the big picture and then move down into the details."

"Good idea," Irene said, pulling a magazine from the top of the stack. "My favorite bathroom is in here." She opened the page to a small bathroom done in crisp white tile with soft green accents and gold fixtures.

Pam studied the photo, then turned down the corner of the page and set the magazine to one side. "Any more?"

Irene showed Pam pictures from four other magazines and three photos she had printed out from her computer.

Pam studied all of them carefully. "All but two of these have white tile," she said.

"I know," Irene said. "I didn't think I would like white tile—I don't want my bathroom to look antiseptic."

"It won't," Pam replied. She opened the magazine to the first photograph Irene had shown her. "The white tile in this bathroom isn't all the same. There are several different tiles, providing textural variety." She traced the photo with her finger, counting the different tiles. "They've used four different tiles, and this long, thin tile has been oriented on the diagonal on one wall in the shower, giving it a completely fresh look."

Irene put on her reading glasses and examined the photo. "Oh. I hadn't noticed that."

"We can do the same in your bathroom. Show me the detail photos."

A server approached their table and cleared her throat.

Pam and Irene both looked up.

"You two ladies are involved in a project," Nicole said.

"I don't want to interrupt, but is there anything I can get you?"

"We should order," Irene said. "Are you hungry?" She looked at Pam.

"I had a late lunch. Can I get an iced tea?" Pam asked.

"Sure. How about you?"

"I'd like the same," Irene said. "I'm sorry that we're taking up your table and only ordering…"

"No worries. We're not busy. You just take your time and enjoy yourselves. I'll get your teas and leave you alone to…" She peered at the papers in front of them. "Fixing up a bathroom?"

"That's right," Irene said.

"I need to work on my spare bathroom," Nicole said. "One of these days," she said as she trailed off.

Pam and Irene were busy sorting photos into categories for tile, faucets, lighting, mirrors, cabinets, and fixtures when the server left their iced teas on the far side of the table. They continued until all the papers were contained in neat stacks.

"This was so helpful," Irene said. "I was feeling scattered when I came in here—like I didn't know what I wanted." She reached across and picked up her tea. "You saw the common themes in the photos I liked."

"You want a crisp, clean look—but not harsh or stark. We'll achieve that with white tile in several textures and patterns. You've got enough wall space to do that effectively." Pam took a sip of her tea. "The photos also add a bit of soft color in accent tile. Half of them have blue tile, while the other half have green."

"I'm not sure how to decide."

"Something will jump out at you when we go to pick

out tile. We'll start with the accent tile and build the rest from there."

"Wouldn't we start with the main white tile?"

Pam shook her head. "All whites are not the same—some are warm toned, leaning to green or yellow, while others are cold with undertones of blue and gray. Picking out white paint or tile is tricky. We'll get the color we want to coordinate with decided on first."

"How did you learn all this? You're really good."

"Maybe it's the hundreds of hours I've spent watching home remodeling shows on TV." She checked her watch. "It's almost five. Duncan's closes at six. Do you want to walk across the square to look at their tile?"

"I can't pick what I want in an hour."

"You won't have to. This is just to get ideas. If there's anything that you think you might like, we can buy a few pieces for you to take home. Sometimes Jed has samples, too."

"That would be fun," Irene said, catching Nicole's eye and making an exaggerated "check" motion with her hand.

Irene began scooping up the magazines and papers to place in the satchel at her feet.

Pam quickly removed two magazines and a handful of papers from the mound in front of Irene. "We'll take these into Duncan's with us."

"Good idea," Irene said.

Nicole brought their check and Irene put a twenty-dollar bill on the tray to pay for the four-dollar tab. "Thanks for letting us park here for so long."

"I'll be right back with your change."

"Keep it," Irene said.

"Gosh, you don't have to do this," Nicole said.

Irene patted her hand.

"Thank you," Nicole said.

Pam rose from the bench.

"All of us here love those posts on Facebook and Instagram about your grandmother's house that you bought and remodeled."

Pam felt the color rise from her collar.

"You're so good!" Nicole waved her hands in front of her as she talked. "We couldn't wait for you to post every day. Two of the breakfast cooks went on about you all the time. You explained things so well and you did stuff anyone could afford."

Irene turned to her daughter, grinning. "She's got the decorator's eye, for sure. I'm so proud of her."

"You should be. We were all so sad when you posted that photo of your entryway light—which is gorgeous, by the way—and said you were done." Her head snapped up, and she took a step back. "Will you start posting again? About this project?" She pointed to the satchel bulging with papers hanging from Irene's shoulder.

"It's not my house," Pam began. "I don't know if…"

"I think that's a great idea!" Irene cut her off. "I'll make sure she posts about my bathroom remodel. It's going to be fabulous!"

"Wait until I tell the others," Nicole looked over her shoulder, toward the kitchen. "They'll be so excited."

"I'm not sure what to say," Pam stammered. "Thank you!"

"We'd better get to Duncan's," Irene said. "We've got a project to start!"

≈

IRENE TURNED a piece of light gray tile over in her hand. "I just don't know," she said, placing it on a vacant spot on a shelf where the item listed on the price sticker was out of stock.

Pam lined it up with the two other accent tile samples her mother had selected—one in soft sea-foam green and one in slate blue. A coordinating white tile abutted each of the colored tile selections.

"I can see what you mean about the differences in white tile." Irene pointed to the samples. "Each of the accent colors requires a different white." She took a step back. "I just can't decide."

"You don't have to," Pam said. "I didn't think you'd even pick out samples this afternoon." She stacked the tiles neatly and cradled them against her chest. "We'll buy all of these and tape them to the wall in your bathroom across from the window. You can see how they look in the space—at all times of day. You'd be surprised how different they'll look in the daytime versus at night."

"That's a good plan."

"Live with them for at least a week. One of these may jump out at you—or you may decide that you don't like any of them."

"I can't imagine that."

"If you do, it's no big deal. We'll return the tile you don't like and pick out something else. Do the same thing all over again. It's easy to change the paint color on the walls, but tile is a more permanent choice."

"I'm excited to see how they look," Irene said. She

followed Pam as she weaved her way around an accordion gate blocking their path.

"Looks like they're doing some construction by your office," Pam said to Jed as she walked up to the checkout and carefully deposited her heavy armload of tile on the counter.

"We're building a small recording studio."

"Really?"

Jed nodded. "You know how I've done that Saturday morning radio show? *Ask Jed Anything?*"

"I listen to it with my airbuds every week—even when I'm helping Mom at the farmer's market. You've taught me so much. I actually called in once."

Jed chuckled. "I remember. We've decided to turn it into a television show. We'll still answer customer questions, but it won't be a call-in format anymore."

"Look at you! Getting all modern and everything."

"We hired a PR firm and they convinced me it's the way to go. We're trying to capitalize on the popularity of home improvement shows. It's not just HGTV anymore. There are others, too."

"I'm so proud of you! You're going to be a TV star."

Jed shook his head. "Not me. I have a face for radio."

"Nonsense! You'll be fine."

"I don't know about that. We're still working on the format of the show."

Pam bounced on her toes. "This is *so* exciting. What are you considering?"

"We might do a segment on a specific remodeling project." His tone was serious. "If you were just starting your house, we'd follow along on your progress."

"I don't think you'd have wanted to do that. I made

more mistakes in the beginning than I care to think about."

"That's part of the authenticity I want to bring to the show," Jed said. "Professionals shouldn't get themselves into trouble, but homeowners do all the time. We want to help people avoid mistakes, of course, but it's important to show people how to fix them when they do happen."

"When are you planning to start airing?" Irene interjected.

"Next month. We've purchased air time."

"Maybe your first segment can be on my bathroom remodel," Irene said, tapping the tile on the counter. "Pam's going to do the work."

"That's a great idea!" Jed looked at Pam. "You're a natural in front of the camera."

"I've got no experience." Pam held out both hands in a stop sign gesture.

"You—and Steve—did that spot on the local news about the Christmas Toy Drive. You were fabulous!" His words came faster as he leaned across the counter toward her. "And tons of people know you from your social media posts about your house remodel. You've already branded yourself as someone who knows about design and the hands-on remodeling process." He looked her in the eye. "You're an influencer."

Pam put her hand to her cheek. It felt warm. This was the second time she'd been called an influencer.

Irene clapped her hands together and brought them to her chest. "I agree, honey. You'd be brilliant."

"You'd help make our new show a success," Jed said. "And we'd pay you."

"Have you both lost your minds?"

"The PR company said we might want to hire a host if the show takes off." He looked from Pam to Irene and back again. "I think we should start off with a host."

Pam stared back, speechless.

"Are these tile samples for your bathroom?" he asked.

Irene nodded.

Jed began wrapping them in heavy paper and placing them in a cardboard box he pulled up from under the counter. "Duncan's will supply all the materials for your remodel. Free of charge."

"You can't do that," Pam said, fishing in her purse for her wallet.

"I most certainly can," Jed said. "We've already budgeted for something like this."

Pam looked up at him. "Well, okay then. In that case, I'll do this segment for your show—for free."

"That won't be necessary."

"It's my final offer. Let's see how my segment works out before you incur any additional expense other than materials for a bathroom."

"If that's what it'll take to get you on board."

Pam nodded.

Jed stuck out his hand, and they shook on it.

"We'd better get these samples home so I can decide," Irene said. "My daughter's going to be a TV star!"

CHAPTER 7

*S*teve shifted in his seat and leaned closer to Pam. The sound on the movie theater screen intensified as six police cars turned on their lights and sirens to pursue the suspect's car. He waited until the surround sound returned to normal decibel levels.

As he leaned in, Steve heard her faint snoring. One look at Pam's face confirmed that she'd fallen into a deep sleep during the blockbuster action film of the season. He watched her rhythmic breathing, then put his arm around her shoulders and kissed her temple.

She bolted awake, pressing herself into her seat back.

"Hey, Sleeping Beauty, I think it's time someone went home and got some shut-eye," he whispered in her ear.

Pam pushed her hair off her forehead. "No. I want to see the rest of the movie."

"We'll watch it when they put it on a streaming service." He placed her hand in his and helped her get to her feet.

They crept quietly out of the theater.

"I fell asleep, didn't I?"

"I'm afraid so." He brought her hand to his lips and kissed it.

"I'm sorry. I know how much you've been looking forward to seeing this." She tugged at his hand and turned toward the theater they'd just left. "Let's go back. I needed to stretch my legs. I'll be fine."

"I don't think so, Princess. You were down for the count, back there."

"Was I... snoring?"

Steve nodded.

"OMG. I'm so sorry. You must be mortified."

"Nobody else heard. It was the tiniest little rumble."

"Oh, brother. Now I'm really embarrassed. I hadn't eaten all day and after that pizza we split for dinner... well... I guess it just did me in."

"I was getting sleepy, myself. As I said, we'll watch it later."

They exited the theater and headed for his SUV.

"Are you working with your mom tomorrow at the market?"

Pam nodded. "This should be the first weekend without rain in a month. The market will be crazy busy. After that, we'll go to Duncan's to order tile for her bathroom. She's made her choice."

"I hope Duncan's follows through with filming you for their first season." They walked slowly, swinging hands in the balmy evening.

"Do you think I should do it? I really don't have any formal education in construction or design."

"Nobody expects you to. You're good—naturally talented. That's all that matters. I think you should try it.

What's the worst that could happen?" He opened her car door.

"I could look like an idiot on TV," Pam said as he slid behind the wheel.

"That's not going to happen." He started the car and turned toward her house. "Oh... I almost forgot. I talked to Carol this morning. Ben says that kid in his class..."

"Larry."

"Doesn't have a dog."

Pam nodded.

Steve glanced at her. "I'm sorry. You were hoping he was the kid who wrote the wish."

"I was, but I'm not surprised. I've thought about it this week, and it seems like the wish would have been written by a younger child."

"That just means your wisher is still out there. You may find him... or her... yet."

"I hope so. I can't shake the feeling that I read that wish because I'm meant to make it come true."

PAM HANDED IRENE a water bottle and took a swig from her own before stowing it under a table. "I'm glad we've had this lull. I can't remember the last time we were this busy."

"I guess everyone's ready to get out of the house and shop after a month of early spring rains." Irene looked at the tablecloths and placemats strewn across the display tables. "It looks like a bomb went off in here."

"It's not even ten o'clock," Pam said. "You'll run out of merchandise if we get another wave of customers." She stood on her tiptoes and looked toward the entrance to the farmer's market. "People are still streaming in."

"I've got three more tubs of merchandise in the back of my car." Irene pulled her keys out of her pocket. "Can you run and get them while I straighten up this mess?"

"Good idea. I'll be right back." Pam grabbed the keys from her mother and began weaving her way through the crowd. When she finally got out into the open, she broke into a run.

Retracing her steps while carrying three large totes in front of her was a slower process. She decided to avoid the throng of shoppers. It would be difficult to quickly skirt the mothers pushing kids in strollers and people walking dogs who were excitedly exploring at the ends of their leashes.

Pam walked along the back of the market stalls at the far end from the entrance, came to an opening, and squeezed herself through. The rental for these spots was far cheaper than what her mother paid for the spot she'd held for at least a decade. These vendors were soliciting for a cause or distributing information. Pam had never wandered into this part of the market. Apparently, most of the other shoppers didn't come here either. There were only a handful of people in this section.

Pam picked up speed and headed for Irene's spot. She was about to turn onto the aisle where her mother's booth was located when she saw the little girl. Short and slight, with a mop of unruly blonde hair tied back with a pink ribbon, she stood behind a table. A small black and tan dog of indiscriminate origin pranced at her side.

A handmade sign was taped to the front of the table. Photos of dogs and cats were pasted into place along an outer circle. On the inside, printed in a familiar childish hand, were the words "Help Stop Killing Them." A glass mason jar sat on the table.

Pam came to a sudden stop, then walked to the table.

A teenaged boy sat on the ground behind the table, intent on his cell phone, his fingers flying across the screen.

The mason jar contained a few dollar bills and a handful of coins.

"Hello," Pam said to the girl. "Tell me about," she pointed to the sign, "this."

"I'm raising money so we can have a no-kill animal shelter here in Linden Falls," the little girl said in a clear voice. She picked up the dog and held him against her chest. "Rusty came from a shelter where they kill dogs and cats that nobody wants. If we hadn't taken him, they might have put him to sleep the next day." She planted a kiss on the top of his head before putting him on the ground again. "He's the best dog ever. I hate that we can't save all the dogs and cats. Somebody could want them. We need to give them a home until they find their forever family."

Pam looked at the little girl with a big voice and an even bigger heart. "I agree with you," she said. She reached into her pocket and cursed silently when she realized she didn't have any money on her.

"My mom has the tablecloth stall up that way," Pam said, gesturing with her head. "I'm bringing these totes of merchandise to her so we can replenish our stock. As soon as I spread these out, I'll come back. I want to give you money for your cause."

A smile exploded from the girl's face. "That'd be great.

I haven't got much so far." She glanced over her shoulder at her brother. "He keeps saying we should go, but I told him we need to stay. I knew someone would come along to help us."

Pam felt tears gathering behind her eyes. "I'll be back. My name is Pam Olson, by the way." She held out her hand to the little girl, who exhibited such a grown-up attitude.

"Laura Thompson," the girl said, shaking her hand.

Pam inhaled sharply. Laura Thompson had to be the person who had written the wish. *I've found her.*

"I'll be back as soon as I can," Pam said. She picked up the totes and pushed her way through the increasingly dense crowd as she made her way to her mother's booth.

Irene was in the middle of bagging up a large order when Pam arrived. The tables were almost empty. Her mother must have been extremely busy in the short time she'd been away.

Pam opened the totes and began restocking the displays with new tablecloths, placemats, table runners, and tea towels. It seemed as if someone picked up each item as soon as she put it down.

The two women worked frantically for the next hour, answering questions, ringing up sales, and taking special orders. They finally sold out of everything.

Irene rested both hands on a table and leaned over it as the last customer left the booth. "I think this is the only time I've ever completely sold out," she said.

Pam grinned at her mother. "Congratulations!"

"I've got a few more totes of inventory at home that wouldn't fit in my car," Irene said, "otherwise I think we could have sold everything I've made. I'm going to have to sew up a storm this week to replace all of this."

"I can come over to help cut fabric after work," Pam said.

"I hate to ask you to do that, but I'll need the help."

"It's a good problem to have," Pam said. "I'm happy for you."

"Thank you. I don't know what I would have done without you."

Pam bit her lip. "Would you mind if I stepped out for a bit?"

"Not at all."

Pam grabbed her purse from under the back table. "I'll be back in a few."

"Take your time. There's no inventory to reload. I just have to take the empty totes and the booth to my car. I'll get it all on my rolling cart."

"You're sure?"

"Of course. Go enjoy the market. You never get to do that, helping me all the time."

"There's this one vendor I want to go see."

"Come to my car when you're done and we'll go to Duncan's to order my tile. And then, I'm going to treat us both to a nice lunch at the Wishing Tree Inn. We've earned it."

Pam hurried out of the booth and made her way to the back of the market. The spot where Laura Thompson had been soliciting donations to fund a no-kill shelter was vacant.

Pam slapped her hands on her thighs in frustration.

The man in the next booth looked at her. "They left

about twenty minutes ago. The boy got impatient and said he wasn't staying with her any longer."

"Do you know if they've been here before?"

The man shook his head. "I've been here every week since the ivory-billed woodpecker showed up in the town tree. I distribute information about local wildlife conservation." He lifted a brochure and handed it to her. "I've never seen them before."

Pam politely took the brochure. "Thank you," she said. "Do you know if she collected much money?"

"The boy—I assume he was her brother—said this had been an enormous waste of time. She'd collected less than twelve dollars and would never reach her goal."

"Oh, gosh," Pam said, bringing her hand to her heart. "That wasn't very nice."

"I thought he might make her cry," the man said, "but that little girl is made of sterner stuff. She told him he didn't know what he was talking about. That all he knew about was stupid video games and that she was going to do something real in this world."

"Wow."

"That's what I thought," the man said. He smiled. "That girl will be a force to reckon with one day."

"I wanted to give her some money," Pam said. "I hope she comes back next week."

"Whether she's here again or not, I know she won't give up." The man nodded to Pam and turned his attention to a couple who walked up to his table.

CHAPTER 8

*S*teve opened the door to the trainer's break room at Linden Falls Fitness and almost collided with Pam. "Where are you headed in such a hurry? You usually have an hour break at this time, so I came looking for you. I thought we could get out of here and grab a coffee."

Pam stopped long enough to put a hand on his chest. "I'd love to, but I've got a client to train. I had to move everyone who was on my schedule for Thursday nights."

Steve raised an eyebrow.

"We start filming this week," Pam said. "I'm demolishing Mom's bathroom. They've scheduled filming from three until ten—or whenever we finish—on Wednesdays and Thursdays." She peered down the hall to make sure no one was coming, then pressed a kiss onto his cheek. "I'd better get going. I don't want to be late. My Thursday clients are doing me a big favor by accommodating my schedule."

Steve stepped aside and watched her hurry away. "I

guess this means we won't be going out on Wednesday nights anymore," he said to her retreating back.

He started into the break room when he heard a familiar voice call his name. He bristled at the simpering tone but forced a smile on his lips and looked over his shoulder at Susan Wilbanks.

"Steve," she said as she walked up to him, smoothing an imaginary wrinkle in her workout clothes that clung to her toned frame like a second skin. "I'd like your advice."

"How can I help?"

"I'm wondering about my son, Sean. He's eleven—such a nice boy—but he's getting in trouble at school." She glanced at Steve's face. "Nothing major. I think he's acting out in response to our separation." Her voice cracked on the last word.

Steve released the handle to the break room door and faced her.

"His dad is completely ignoring him," Susan said. "Doesn't spend any time with him. I think Sean's trying to get his attention."

"Have you talked to your husband?"

"We're not exactly on speaking terms right now," she said.

"I really don't even know Sean," Steve began. "I'm not sure what I could do to help."

"I was wondering if you could recommend an activity for him to get involved in? A sport or something like that. I believe those are so helpful for kids." She moved closer to him.

"You must know that I run the youth soccer league that plays all its games on Saturday nights. I've been doing it for years. Everybody in town knows that."

Susan's eyes grew big. "I can't believe I forgot. Of course, I remember now!"

"Does Sean like soccer?"

"Of course he does."

"It's a great sport for kids," Steve said. "All the running keeps them fit and being part of a team teaches essential life skills. Injuries are low and anyone can pick up the skills to become a good player." He was warming to his subject. "Plus, they play soccer in clubs, at school, and in intramural teams all year long. Why don't you bring him on Saturday night? He can observe and I'll take him around. If he's interested, I can assign him to a team."

"You'd do that for me?" She leaned toward him.

Steve took a step away, pressing his back against the door to the break room. "Sure. I think soccer would be very good for him—especially right now. We meet at the fields by the high school."

"I don't know how to thank you," she said, planting a lingering kiss on his cheek.

Steve turned his head aside and pushed past Susan. He didn't see Pam walking with her client at the other end of the hall, her gaze fixed on the scene that had just transpired.

"I'll see you Saturday," Susan gushed.

"You can drop Sean off with me at five and pick him up at eight," Steve said. "And now, I've got to go."

CHAPTER 9

*P*am arrived at her mother's house at two-thirty on Wednesday afternoon. The driveway was filled with two cargo vans, their back doors flung open. A handful of people scurried from the vans to the house, unloading cameras, sound booms, lights, and other equipment. Three additional vehicles were parked in front.

She proceeded down the block and found a spot along the curb three houses from Irene's. Pam checked her reflection in her rearview mirror. She'd put on eyeliner and mascara before she'd left the house at five that morning. Her hair was neatly pulled back in a ponytail that extended out the back of her Duncan's Hardware monogrammed baseball cap. She'd bought a new long-sleeved white T-shirt and wore a clean pair of jeans. From what she'd seen on the home improvement shows she'd watched, she looked like the consummate host.

Pam hoisted her purse onto her shoulder and headed for her mom's. As she got closer, she observed people running in and out of the house with their oversized loads.

She hadn't realized that there would be so much involved in filming this project. She smiled and shook her head. She'd posted numerous videos on her social media accounts, all done on her cell phone camera. Clearly, this show was a much bigger deal.

Irene stepped onto the porch as Pam came up the walkway. She motioned to her daughter to hurry and join her.

Pam picked up her pace. When she got to the edge of the porch, her eyebrows shot up.

Irene giggled at her daughter's reaction. "I'm going to be on-screen for this first segment," she said. "This being my house and all. They asked if I wanted them to do my hair and makeup. The makeup artist said you have to wear way more on the screen than you'd ever put on in real life." She turned her head from side to side. "What do you think?"

Pam stared at her mother. She'd never seen her with black eyeliner or coral lips, but it was artfully applied. "You look great!" she said, not wanting to dampen her mother's enthusiasm. "I like what they've done with your hair."

Irene lifted one hand to run it over the sleek bob that the stylist had coaxed out of her unruly curls. "They've been asking when you were going to get here."

"Nobody told me about hair and makeup," Pam said. "I'm just here to take down tile and remove cabinets."

Irene caught and held her eye.

"I put on makeup this morning," Pam replied, waving her hand dismissively.

"And ran a comb through your hair, I see," Irene said. "Follow me. Let's allow the professionals to decide if you need any help with your appearance."

Thirty minutes later, Pam looked in a hand mirror and hardly recognized herself. While the makeup artist had applied foundation, powders, blushers, bronzers, and a dozen different eye products, the hair stylist had unleashed her hair from the baseball cap and ponytail. It now hung around her shoulders in gentle curls.

Irene, who had been hovering in the back of the room, now spoke. "You look like a Breck girl," she said, clapping her hands together.

Pam and the makeup artist turned to her with quizzical expressions.

"Those were some of the most iconic shampoo models of the nineteen sixties and seventies."

The stylist grinned. "That's high praise, indeed."

"I'm doing demo work—you know that, don't you? I'll get filthy. My makeup will smudge, and my hair won't hold this curl." Pam picked up a lock of hair and allowed it to drop back to her shoulder.

"That's why we're here," the stylist said, holding up the curling iron she'd used on Pam's hair.

"We'll be on you like moths to a flame between takes. It's our job to make sure you look flawless on camera."

Pam swallowed hard and turned to Irene. "Wow," she said. "This is the real deal."

"I know," Irene said, shifting her weight from foot to foot.

"Are you sure you're okay with all of this?" Pam pointed toward the bathroom that was to be the subject of the show. "With all these people in your home, two nights a week? Especially with the sewing you need to do to replenish your inventory."

"Are you kidding? This is the most fun I've had in ages. And don't you worry about my sewing. Leona Mills is helping me and she's quite good."

Pam stared at her mother. "You've got it all figured out."

"I'm going to do anything I can to help my TV-star daughter." She beamed at Pam.

"Ladies," a man spoke to them from the bedroom door. "We're ready for you."

THE STYLIST REMOVED the curling iron and yet again arranged a strand of Pam's chestnut hair at her throat.

It felt awkward and Pam wished it was Vera standing behind her. Vera had done her hair for ages and knew just how to make it behave and always made her feel at ease.

The makeup artist dabbed at the perspiration on her upper lip. "I know it's hard to have both of us fussing over you between takes," the makeup artist said.

"Ready?" called the director. When the camera operator gave him a thumbs-up, Marty Beckman, a stocky man in his mid-fifties with thinning hair and a kind face, looked back to Pam.

Pam arranged her features into a pleasant expression as both the stylist and makeup artist melted into the shadows.

The assistant clapped the clapperboard together and called, "Action."

Pam froze, her smile plastered on her face, and stared into the camera.

"Cut." Marty walked up and put his hand on her shoulder. "Just relax. You and your mom were great together in the intro."

"I'm so sorry," Pam said. "Standing here, in front of the camera by myself, feels so different."

"You'll get used to it. Everybody feels nervous at first." He patted her shoulder reassuringly. "We got terrific footage of you in the intro demolishing the tile in the shower."

"I wondered about that," Pam said. "My hair was falling into my face, driving me crazy. I could barely see what I was doing. Can't I tie it back? I mean—honestly— who does construction work with flawlessly styled hair?" She glanced toward the corner of the room where the stylist was scrolling on her phone.

"Television—even reality TV—isn't all real. People like the myth that their celebrities are perfect."

"I'm not a celebrity," Pam said.

"You will be," Marty replied. "Are you ready to try it again?"

Pam drew a deep breath and released it slowly before she nodded.

"All you have to do is tell the audience how you're going to prep the walls for the new tile."

"Got it," Pam said. She squared her shoulders and lifted her chin to the camera.

The assistant leaned in and clapped the clapperboard.

Pam stumbled over the first few words. They stopped and started again. On the fifth take, Marty finally indicated he was satisfied.

"Okay, everybody. That's a wrap for today. Good work. The first day is always the hardest—everyone is finding their footing." He glanced at Pam. "See you here tomorrow. You'll be taking out the old tub and toilet, right?"

"Yes. Duncan's is sending over one of their employees to help me."

"A piece of advice? Don't replay tonight over and over in your mind. It'll do you no good. Get a good night's sleep and we'll hit it again tomorrow."

Can he read my mind? Pam felt exactly like she had in high school when her mother had caught her planning to sneak out of the house with her girlfriends. "Of course," she said. "I'll do just that."

IRENE SHUT and locked her front door as the last van pulled out of her driveway.

"Do you need help with anything?" Pam asked, looking around the house that had been a beehive of activity only a few minutes earlier.

"No," Irene said. "They cleaned up after themselves really well. Everything's back in place."

"It's almost ten. I'd better get home to feed Leopold."

"That cat of yours can wait another half hour. I'll bet you haven't eaten since lunch."

Pam swallowed hard.

"Since breakfast?" Irene asked. "I was just going to scramble myself a couple of eggs. Let me make some for you, too. You can handle the toast."

"I'm starved," Pam admitted, following her mother into the kitchen.

"I've got just enough of my homemade sourdough left for a big slice for each of us." Irene pointed to the old-fashioned bread box on the counter.

Pam pulled out the bread knife from the drawer while Irene got eggs and butter from the refrigerator.

"What did you think?" Pam asked.

"The entire process is way more involved than I imagined," Irene said as she cracked eggs into a pan. "It's all rather exciting. And I like what they did with my hair and makeup." She checked her reflection in the kitchen window. "I took a bunch of selfies so I can recreate the look if I ever go anywhere fancy."

"That's a smart idea," Pam said. "They did a nice job. You were great on camera." The bread popped up, and she buttered it.

"You were, too," Irene said. "It was as if we were having an actual conversation. Like we are now."

"That felt very natural." Pam rested her wrist on the counter, butter knife pointed to the ceiling. "But when it came time for me to talk to the camera—all by myself—I was a complete disaster."

"Didn't the director say that you'll get the hang of it?"

Pam nodded. "I'm not so sure. While they fuss with my hair and makeup, I go over what I'm going to say. I think I'm all set, but the moment he snaps that clapper thing, my brain turns to mush."

Irene put a large spoonful of egg on a plate and handed it to Pam.

Pam placed a piece of toast next to the eggs and

handed the plate back to Irene before doing the same on the next plate.

Pam carried her dinner to the kitchen table and sat, slumping against the seat back. "I can't stop rerunning it in my head; what I should have said and the gestures I should have made. Instead, I stood in front of the camera like I was playing statues." She moaned and put her head in her hands.

"Marty told you not to do this. He said you need to get a good night's sleep and you'll be fine tomorrow."

Pam shrugged.

"He's made a career of filming things for television. He knows what he's talking about."

"You think so? I'll be better tomorrow?"

"I'm sure of it. This was just first-day jitters. He wouldn't lie to you."

Pam lifted her head.

"Now, let's eat before this gets cold," Irene said, picking up her fork and digging into the modest meal. "I'll make chicken noodle soup in the crock-pot tomorrow, so we have something better when we're done filming."

CHAPTER 10

*J*ed smiled as he saw Marty Beckman's name on the screen of his phone. The employee he'd sent to Irene's the day before to help Pam with the removal of the tub, sink, and toilet had just come in to work and reported that they'd finished filming at eleven the night before. Jed was eager to hear how the director thought things were going.

"Marty," Jed said. "How's the show coming?"

"The first week's film is off to editing," Marty replied. "I think we got some great footage. Pam's a hard worker and she knows what she's doing."

"I knew it. The guy I sent over to help said that she's careful in the way she works—and smart and efficient. That's exactly what I want in a host."

"There may be one problem," Marty said. He took a deep breath.

"What's that? What do you need?"

"She struggles in front of the camera by herself. She's

dynamite when she's got someone else to play off of, but…"

"It's early days, isn't it? You're just getting started. She'll loosen up."

"That's what I'm hoping," Marty said. "I wanted to mention it to you, in case we need to… go another direction."

"What does that mean?" Jed straightened in his desk chair and leaned forward.

"Don't be alarmed. I was thinking we could bring in another host, so she'd have someone to talk to on-screen."

"Like these couples that do the HGTV shows?"

"Exactly. I know she's not married, so I thought maybe you could be on-screen with her. You're the sponsor, after all."

"Nope. No way," Jed said. "If you think she gets tongue-tied, I'd be ten times worse."

"We'll see how things go next week," Marty said. "Maybe I'm worrying about nothing. In the meantime, think about someone we could bring in as a co-host."

"Will do." Jed hung up and sank into his chair. A smile soon spread across his face. He had the ideal candidate. Whether he could convince him to take the part was another matter.

PAM RELEASED the tendril from her curling iron and arranged it on her shoulders. She flipped the strand and twisted it, staring at her reflection in her mirror. No matter how much she fussed, she couldn't achieve the look that the stylist had the prior two nights.

She unplugged the curling iron, swiped peachy gloss over her lips, and went to the kitchen to feed Leopold. She'd no sooner set the bowl on the floor for her always-hungry cat when she heard Steve's car in the driveway.

Pam positioned a turquoise wrap around her shoulders and picked up her black clutch from the entry table. She caught her reflection in the mirror above the table. Even without professionally styled hair, she looked striking in a slim black sheath, the colorful wrap popping against her fair complexion.

She heard Steve on the steps and opened the door before he could knock.

He stopped and looked at her, silhouetted in the doorway. "You look stunning," he said. "Stunning," he repeated.

"You're mighty handsome, yourself, in that blue suit, white shirt, and silver tie."

Steve extended his hand, holding out an enormous bouquet of yellow roses, tipped with pink.

"They're lovely! My favorite roses," Pam said. "You remembered. Bistro Claudine—roses—what're we celebrating?" She motioned for him to follow her inside. "I need to put these in water."

"The end of your first week of filming, of course. I figured we should get out of our workout clothes and do it up right."

"I'm not entirely sure there's anything to celebrate." Pam opened a cabinet and pointed to a cut-glass vase on the top shelf.

Steve reached up and retrieved it for her. "Why do you say that?"

Pam ran water into the vase and began snipping the

end of each stem under running water before placing it into the vase.

Steve watched her and waited patiently.

"I'm not a natural in front of a camera."

"Nonsense. You're made for this gig."

"I'm a good home remodeler. I know how to achieve a champagne look on a beer budget. But you turn a camera on me, and my mind turns to mush. I can't make my lips move."

"You did great on the toy drive interview. You just have to get your sea legs under you. Anyone would."

Pam carried the vase of flowers to her dining room table. "These are lovely. Thank you."

"I figured you could enjoy them all weekend." He leaned toward her and gave her a quick kiss on the lips. "I know about not messing up a woman's lipstick," he said. "And now, we'd better get going. Our reservation is in fifteen minutes."

He headed west, and they drove into the setting sun. The clouds that had made the spring day overcast, now authored a spectacular sunset of oranges, golds, and pinks. Steve glanced at Pam, who appeared more relaxed than he'd seen her all week. He opened the moon roof for the short drive and the balmy air embraced them. She relaxed in her seat, taking in the vibrant spring green of the trees along Main Street.

They arrived at the restaurant and were seated by a window overlooking a courtyard with raised beds of herbs that were used in the cuisine. They ordered wine and an appetizer of burrata and arugula, with tomato jam on crostini, and handed their menus to the server.

"You're really bothered by it, aren't you?"

"This television thing?" Pam asked. "I just can't shake this feeling that it's not quite right for me."

"What has the director told you?"

"That I need to get used to being on camera. That I'll get better at it."

"Well, then…"

"Except I don't think he really believes that. He's having doubts about me."

"I'm sure that's not true."

The server brought their appetizer and set it on the table between them, together with two smaller plates. "Are you ready to order your entrees?"

Pam selected salmon with risotto and Steve picked a balsamic-glazed pork chop with fingerling potatoes.

Steve leaned across the table when the server left and took her hand. "If it's not working, the director will tell you. In the meantime, why don't you just do what they tell you to do and see what happens? This isn't your day job, you know. Nothing bad is going to happen to you—and you still get to remodel Irene's bathroom on someone else's dime."

Pam laughed. "That's true. When you put it like that, it doesn't seem so dire."

"Excellent." He spread a crostino with cheese, added a smear of jam, and balanced chopped arugula on top before placing it on her plate. "Why don't you tell me about the remodel? Where are you in the process?"

As they worked their way through the delicious meal, Pam filled him in on her progress and the plans she and Irene had made.

"When will the first episode air?" Steve asked as the server brought them a warm brownie topped with homemade vanilla bean ice cream and drizzled with sea-salted caramel. He set the decadent dessert between them, flanked by two spoons.

"Four weeks from tomorrow. *Wishes of Home*—that's the name of the show—will air at ten on Saturday mornings. We film again Wednesday and Thursday of next week, so they'll always be filming four weeks ahead of schedule."

"That gives them time to edit."

"Exactly."

A smile slipped over Steve's lips. "I want to watch the first episode with you," he said, his eyes telegraphing earnestness.

"That's so sweet of you," Pam said. "Irene and I will work her booth at the farmer's market that Saturday morning. She's been busier than ever this spring, so I'll record it to watch at my house as soon as we get home. You can join us."

"It's all set, then." Steve picked up his spoon, inserting it into the ice cream. He pressed down, scooping up a portion of the warm brownie and soft ice cream.

Pam joined in, scooping up a huge bite.

He eyed her spoonful, then raised one eyebrow.

"What?" She smiled playfully. "We can't let this melt."

"Good point." He took another spoonful as they both leaned into the task.

CHAPTER 11

"Come see us again," Pam said, handing a woman her package containing eight placemats with a coordinating table runner and napkins. "Everything in here," she gestured to the booth, "is one of a kind. Mom makes new items every week."

"I come to the market on the last Saturday of every month and I'll be sure to check back. I'm so excited about using these." She held up her parcel. "I'm having company for dinner tomorrow night and they'll be lovely on my table."

"Would you mind sharing a photo of your tablescape with me?" Pam pulled a business card out of the back pocket of her jeans. "I'd love to post it on our social media."

"Really?" The woman tucked the card into a slot inside her purse. "I'd like that."

"Be sure to give me your social media handles and I'll tag you." Pam smiled at the woman while glancing at the booth behind her. "Would you excuse me? This is the first time all morning we haven't been knee deep in customers. I need to take a break."

"Gosh, no problem," the woman said. "If you need to head to the ladies' room, go for it." She exited the booth.

Pam nodded but didn't correct the woman's assumption. She was going to look for Laura Thompson and her booth.

Irene was at the front of the booth, bent over a table, straightening the display of placements and coordinating items that Pam's customer had left in disarray.

Pam caught her mother's eye and mouthed the words, "Be right back."

Irene nodded and Pam took off at a fast clip toward the far side of the market. She increased her pace as the crowds thinned. She spotted the man with the wildlife conservation booth who she'd talked to the prior week. Her heart sank as she saw that the table next to him was occupied by two young women soliciting interest in a mommy-and-me yoga group.

She forced herself onward, speed walking up and down the aisles in this less popular section of the market. Laura and her brother might have set up their table in a different spot.

After another five minutes of searching, she reluctantly concluded that they weren't there. She'd also been gone from Irene's booth for far too long. It was time to head back.

Pam retraced her steps. When she got to the wildlife conservation booth, she walked up to the man. "Hi," she said, "I talked to you last week."

"About the girl raising money for an animal shelter? I remember you."

Pam smiled at him. "I was looking for her. Have you seen her?"

He shook his head. "I have a feeling last week was the one and only time we're going to see that little girl and her brother here. She's probably trying to find another way to raise the money."

Pam had come to the same conclusion, but hearing his words weighed heavily on her. She nodded to the man and returned to her mother's booth.

Irene was doing her best to answer questions simultaneously from two different shoppers while adding up an order and taking payment from another.

Pam stepped in to assist one of the women trying to decide between placemats or a tablecloth. She and her mother worked nonstop until the market closed at one o'clock.

Pam was helping Irene load unsold inventory, tables, and the booth into the back of Irene's SUV when she caught sight of the back of a young girl with an unruly shock of blonde hair tied with a pink ribbon.

Recognition surged through her. This girl, crossing the street and walking away from the market, had to be Laura Thompson. Pam shoved the table she was holding into the car and took off after the youngster. "Be right back," she said to Irene for the second time that morning.

Pam reached the street corner as the light turned red.

The girl, who appeared to be accompanied by a tall, lanky teen, had just stepped onto the sidewalk on the opposite side.

Pam felt her pulse quicken.

The girl and boy continued walking straight toward the public parking lot that serviced the square.

Pam kept them in her sight, glad that she was tall. She glanced at the traffic light, which had turned yellow in the opposite direction. She'd be able to cross soon.

Three young women, pushing strollers and holding the hands of toddlers, walked behind the girl and boy, obliterating them from view.

Pam rose to her tiptoes and searched the pedestrians on the other side of the street. Her mouth grew increasingly dry as she feared she'd lost them.

When the light turned green, she ran across the street and proceeded after them. She reached the end of the block and stopped, turning her head in each direction. The girl and boy were nowhere to be seen. She'd lost them.

Pam ran her fingers through her hair. Why was finding Laura Thompson proving to be so elusive, and why was she so intent on finding her anyway?

She retraced her steps, this time walking with less determination. Pam was passing Doc's Fountain when the door opened and a tall boy emerged, followed closely by the girl with unruly blonde hair tied with a pink ribbon. Each of them was clutching ice cream cones—his with three scoops and hers with two.

Pam felt winded—as if someone had punched her in the stomach. It wasn't them. The boy and girl weren't Laura Thompson and her brother.

She moved to the side of the building and rested her back against the brick, watching as the top scoop fell off the girl's ice cream cone and splatted onto the sidewalk. The child's face clouded over and she drew a deep breath, but before she could let out a wail, the boy took her hand and marched them both back inside Doc's.

He must be buying her another scoop of ice cream, Pam surmised. She entered the flow of pedestrian traffic and rejoined her mother as Irene was stowing the last items in her SUV.

"I wondered where you went." She looked at her daughter.

"I thought I saw someone I wanted to talk to. Turns out, it wasn't them."

"You look pretty crestfallen. Did they owe you money or something?"

Pam laughed. "No. Nothing like that." She closed the hatchback. "I'm going to run into Town Square Books, then I'll come to your house. I want to clean out the rest of the debris from your bathroom."

"Don't you need to wait for the film crew?"

Pam shook her head. "We'll be filming preparation for your new shower next week. I have to get everything ready."

"You've worked hard all week, and we were so busy this morning. Why don't you take the afternoon off and do it tomorrow?"

"It may take me all of today and tomorrow," Pam said. "I'll be doing this project much quicker than usual now that we're on TV."

"I didn't realize that. I hope it won't be too much for you."

"I'll manage."

"What about time with Steve? Aren't you going out with him tonight?"

Pam shook her head. "We saw each other last night. We only ever go out on Friday nights—never Saturday."

Irene swung her head to Pam but didn't comment.

"It's odd, I know," Pam said.

"Everything all right between you?"

"As far as I know. He took me to Bistro Claudine last night and brought me my favorite roses—to celebrate my first week on TV."

"That sounds very thoughtful," Irene said, nodding approvingly.

"All I know is that I need to put my head down and work on your bathroom."

Irene reached out and rubbed her daughter's arm. "I'll stop at the market for a couple of nice steaks. If you're sacrificing all your free time to work on my bathroom, the least I can do is fix a nice dinner. You've got my key. You can let yourself in and get started if I'm not home before you get there."

Irene pulled away and Pam crossed the street to Town Square Books.

CHAPTER 12

The door to the bookstore was propped open by a large pot of peonies. Pam paused to admire them when an older woman and a young girl, clutching a shopping bag bearing the Town Square Books logo, exited the shop.

"Lovely, aren't they?" The woman smiled at Pam. "My yard was full of them before I moved to Aspen Grove. Grew like weeds."

"They sure are. I'm thinking of planting some at my house."

"You won't be sorry. They'll come up year after year."

The little girl shifted the heavy bag in her arms.

"We'd better be on our way. I've only got my grand-daughter for a few more hours before her parents pick us up. We always go to Doc's Fountain for maple creemees when we're done here."

"That sounds like a wonderful idea." Pam stepped aside as the pair exited and headed for Doc's.

The store was empty except for Paige who was leaning

over a square table in the front, tidying ˯
Vermont-themed books. There were tourist guid˯
books, glossy decorating magazines, folding maps, ˯
even boxes of note cards with drawings of the Wishing
Tree depicted in each season.

"Hi, Paige," Pam said, coming to stand beside her.

Paige startled. "I didn't hear you come in," she said,
bringing her hand to her heart. "We've been slammed all
day. This is the first break I've had."

"Mom was busy, too." Pam picked up a box of the note
cards and turned it over, reading the text on the back.
"You made these?"

Paige nodded and reached for them. "Just a little something I thought I'd try…"

Pam pulled her hand back. "They're beautiful. I'm
buying them for myself. I think I'll put one of each design
in a collage frame and hang it in my foyer."

"Really?" Paige couldn't suppress the grin that light-
ened her tired expression.

"Absolutely!" Pam walked to the register and set the
box of note cards to one side. "I'm also looking for… self-
help books."

"We have a whole section." Paige began walking
toward the back of the store. "Are you after anything in
particular?"

Pam pursed her lips, then sighed heavily. "I don't think
I'm doing a very good job as the host of *Wishes of Home*.
Marty and Jed tell me I'll get the hang of it, but I'm not so
sure. I don't even know what kind of book I'd need."

Paige walked to the middle of an aisle and pointed to
an entire section. "These are all books on public speaking. I'd start here." She pulled out a book by Dale

Carnegie. "He's the grand master in this field. We've got at least a dozen of his titles. There are books about TED talks and lots of other guides, too." She cocked her head to one side. "You know that a huge percentage of people are terrified at the thought of public speaking, don't you? That's why we've devoted so much space to the subject."

"I'd heard that, yes. I guess talking on camera is sort of like public speaking."

"Definitely," Paige said. She turned as Gladys, who had been softly snoring in the back of the store after the busy morning, ambled toward them. "I'll leave you in Gladys's capable… paws," she said. "Take your time and browse as much as you like."

Paige returned to her display table while Pam dropped to one knee to greet Gladys. When she'd finished the belly rub that Gladys insisted upon, Pam stood and carefully perused the books in front of her. Thirty minutes later, she approached the register with an armload of books.

Paige rang them up. "You've selected the best of the best," she commented. "You'll feel better when you've read these."

"I hope so. Which one do you recommend I start with?"

"*How to Develop Self-Confidence and Improve Public Speaking.* You can't go wrong with that."

"Then I'll start there. Thank you for the recommendations."

Gladys pressed her muzzle against Pam's leg and she leaned over to scratch behind Gladys's ears. "Did you get my note cards?"

Paige slipped the box of note cards into the sack with

the large stack of hardbacks Pam had bought. "None of your books were on sale, so I'm including them for free."

"You don't have to do that!"

"I want to." Paige handed the heavy carrier bag to Pam. "Good luck. You're going to do great."

"Thank you." Pam gave Gladys one last pat goodbye and headed out of the store.

IRENE STOOD in the doorway of her master bathroom and looked at her daughter as she cut away sheetrock where the shower's tile had been. "It's after six," Irene said. "Shall I throw the steaks on the grill?"

Pam rocked back on her heels and set her saw aside. She deposited the contents of her dustpan in the five-gallon bucket bearing the Duncan's Hardware name and logo. "That'd be great. I'm starved—and exhausted. I'm going to call it quits for tonight."

"I think that's wise," Irene said.

"I'll come back tomorrow to finish getting ready for new backer board." She got to her feet and swept her hands down her jeans, raising a cloud of drywall dust.

Irene took a step back. "Take off your T-shirt and jeans and I'll put them in the washer. You can wear my robe during dinner. I'll have them dry by the time you need to leave."

Pam stripped out of her clothes. "Good idea. I'll bring some spare work clothes tomorrow."

"My robe's hanging in the other bathroom," Irene said as she made her way to the laundry room with the dirty clothes.

Pam found the robe and snuggled herself into it, taking comfort in the faint scent of Shalimar—her mother's favorite perfume—that clung to it. She checked her reflection in the mirror. Her hair was chalky with dust and her face was gritty with it. She would need to shower as soon as she got home—if she could stay awake that long. Pam splashed water on her face and tucked an escaped tendril back into her ponytail.

Irene was tossing a green salad with homemade balsamic dressing when Pam entered the kitchen. Two steaks sat on the counter, resting. A baked potato was on each of their plates, with butter, sour cream, and chopped green onions in bowls on the table, at the ready for fixings. "Sit," Irene ordered. "I'll bring your food. You look like you're about to collapse. No wonder, as hard as you're working."

Pam sank into a chair. "It's not as bad as all that. I'll get a second wind after I eat."

Irene placed the larger of the two steaks onto a plate with the biggest potato and set it in front of Pam. She followed with a bowl of salad and a tall glass of ice water.

"Thanks, Mom." Pam took a long drink.

Irene served herself and joined her daughter at the table. "I thought that everything you did would be captured on film."

Pam shook her head as she attacked her salad. "The show will hit the highlights of the remodel. They've divided it into eight segments, with a distinct task for each week. In between each one, I'm supposed to do the work required to make sure we're ready for that segment."

"All by yourself?" Irene cut into her steak, eyeing the warm red center. "Is yours cooked okay?"

Pam sliced through the middle of her steak. "Just the way I like it." She took a bite. "I did all the work when I remodeled the bathrooms at my house. The difference is I had more time to get things done—I wasn't on a filming deadline." She smiled at Irene. "The only new thing with your bathroom is the curbless shower."

"I don't need that," Irene began.

"It's the latest thing and Duncan's wants to showcase it. It's also a great idea—you won't have to step over anything to get into the shower."

"Won't water from the shower run all over the bathroom?"

"Not if the floor is properly prepared. Duncan's is sending an expert plumber for this week's show to get the floor just right. All I need to do is talk about it on camera." She sighed heavily.

"That's good, isn't it? You'll have some help."

"I'd rather do the work than talk about it."

"Are you still nervous about being on camera?"

Pam nodded, lifting eyes filled with misery to her mother.

Irene leaned across the table and took her daughter's hand. "Listen to me. You've only been at this for one week. Give it time. That's what Marty told you. You've got this."

Pam nodded and tried to smile.

"All you need is a good night's sleep and everything will seem better in the morning."

Pam squeezed her mother's hand. "I'm sure you're right. I'll feel better after I've finished getting the space ready for next week's filming, too."

"About that—why don't you ask Jed for some additional help from the store? It seems like you've bitten off more than you can chew."

"We'll see," Pam replied, cleaning her plate. "I think you're right. I need to get some sleep. I'll head home now and be sawing logs before nine." She stood and took her plate to the sink. She reached for the dishwasher handle, but Irene stopped her.

"I'll take care of all of this. Get out of here. You've done enough for one day."

Pam put her arms around her mother and kissed the top of her head. "Thank you for such a delicious dinner. I'll see you first thing in the morning."

"Why don't you sleep in?"

"I get up so early during the week that six is sleeping late for me."

Irene took Pam's face in her hands. "I'm serious. I don't want you working yourself to the bone on my account."

Pam hugged her mother and headed out the door.

CHAPTER 13

"Hey, buddy. I hear you're interested in soccer?" Steve rose from his desk and walked to the doorway where the sullen boy stood next to his mother.

Sean shrugged.

"He most certainly is," Susan gushed. "Aren't you, Sean? Mr. Turner is going to introduce you to all the kids."

Sean glanced at Steve, his expression guarded.

"I'm Steve," he said, holding out his hand.

The boy stepped forward and shook it, looking at the ground.

"I'd love to show you around and let you get a feel for our program. It doesn't matter whether you're a great player or a novice. All we're after is to support each other and have fun."

Sean nodded.

"Have you played much?"

"Not really."

"Doesn't matter. This is the place to learn." He put his hand on Sean's shoulder and they walked toward a door that led to the playing fields.

Susan followed behind.

"Why don't you leave Sean with me? I'm sure you've got something else to do." He looked at Sean. "Would that be okay with you?"

Sean nodded vigorously.

"Oh... okay," Susan said. "When would you like me to come back?"

"We finish here at eight." He looked at Sean again.

"Sure," Sean said. "I'm cool with that."

"Then I'll be back at eight. Call me if you need anything. And be a good boy."

Sean rolled his eyes, and Steve laughed.

"We'll be fine. See you later."

Susan watched Steve and Sean walk through the door, her head tilted to one side. The faraway expression in her eyes signaled she was thinking of other things.

SUSAN WALKED SLOWLY to her car, disappointed that Steve hadn't even noticed her new outfit, the cropped sweater and leggings she'd paid a fortune for online.

She unlocked her car and slid behind the wheel. She sat there, watching other parents drop off kids.

A woman arrived in an older compact car and walked a boy and girl into the facility. When she returned, her car wouldn't start. She opened the hood.

Susan sank down in her seat, hoping the woman wouldn't see her and ask for help.

A truck arrived to drop off an older boy. The driver noticed the woman and pulled into the parking spot next to her. He spoke to the woman, pulled out a set of jumper cables that he used to connect their batteries, and got her car started.

Susan watched as the woman fumbled in her purse and pulled out money, which the man refused. Susan sat bolt upright, suddenly optimistic with a new idea.

She exited the lot and made the short drive to her house. She pulled into the garage and donned an old jacket hanging on a peg by the back door.

She opened her hatchback, rolled aside the floor mat, and wrangled the donut tire out of position, allowing it to drop to the garage floor. She rolled it to one side before carefully repositioning the rear floor mat.

Susan entered her house to use the bathroom and touch up her makeup. She applied an extra layer of lipstick and blotted it, grinning at herself in the mirror. She discarded the tissue with the blood-red swath and checked the time on the clock in her hallway. It was after six-thirty. She hung the old jacket on its peg and set out for the soccer fields.

Susan was the first parent to arrive for parent pick up. She took the tire pressure gauge from her glove box and began implementing her plan.

By seven ten, Susan was seated in her Range Rover, scrolling through social media on her phone. The right front tire was flat as a pancake.

The parking lot was busy from seven-thirty until eight, as parents arrived and children ran in groups to waiting cars, their high-spirited voices filling the air.

Susan got out of the Range Rover when the activity

died down and walked toward Steve's office. She intercepted Steve and Sean on their way to the parking lot.

"We were just coming to find you," Steve said.

Susan pasted her most maternal smile on her lips. "How was it, Sean? Did you have fun?"

"I had the best time!" Sean raced up to his mother. "I'm gonna be on a team with a couple of kids I know from school."

"That's wonderful." Susan kept her eyes on Steve.

"He did very well," Steve said. "He'll be a great player in no time."

"I'm invited to practice with them tomorrow afternoon." Sean bubbled with excitement. "Can I go?"

"Sure. As long as I can get my tire fixed." Susan pulled a long face.

"What's going on?" Steve asked.

"My tire's flat," Susan said. "I noticed it when I got out of the car. I've called roadside assistance. They'll come change the tire for me, but they can't get here for another couple of hours."

"I'm sure I can change it for you, so you don't have to wait," Steve said.

"Really?" Susan gushed. "That would be so nice. I know Sean's tired. I'd like to get home."

They walked up to the Range Rover and Steve glanced at the tire. "It sure is flat. Can you release the hatchback for me? I'll get the spare."

Susan clicked a button on her key fob and the hatchback opened. She watched as Steve searched for the donut tire that wasn't there.

"You don't have a spare," Steve said, stepping aside and closing the hatchback. "Did you know that?"

Susan shook her head. "This is a new car, too."

"You should go back to the dealership—insist they give you one."

"Can I drive home on it, do you think?"

"Absolutely not. You'll ruin your rims."

Susan made a show of pulling her phone out of her purse. "I'll call an Uber. We don't need to hold you up. I'll come back tomorrow to deal with all of this." She sighed as she scrolled through her screen.

"I'm happy to give you a ride home."

"That would be so nice of you!" Susan looked at him coyly. "Don't you have somewhere else to be tonight? An eligible bachelor like you?"

"I have time to drop the two of you off," Steve said, a stiffness creeping into his manner. "Come on, Sean. You can tell your mother all about tonight." He turned and led the way to his SUV.

Sean bounded after him as Susan strutted along behind.

CHAPTER 14

*P*am drove down Main Street, the Wishing Tree Inn to her right, and the square, now deserted after the busy farmer's market that morning, on her left. The top of the Wishing Tree was silhouetted against the night sky, majestic and solid. A handful of wishes hung from its low branches, twisting in the gentle breeze.

She wondered if she'd ever run into Laura Thompson again. She was convinced that Laura was the author of the wish Pam had rescued from the storm—the one that longed for a no-kill animal shelter in Linden Falls. The heart-wrenching words had looked tear-stained from the rain. She didn't know how she could do it, but she wanted to make Laura's wish come true.

Pam was easing into the right lane to complete the short drive to her house when a familiar SUV approached from the opposite direction.

Her breath caught in her throat. Pam slowed to a crawl and turned to stare as it passed to her left.

The driver was a tall, dark-haired man. She'd know that profile anywhere. It was Steve Turner. And he wasn't alone in the car.

Pam continued to the end of the block, her thoughts roiling like rapids after a spring rain. There had been a woman in the car with him.

Her mouth tasted sour, and she swallowed bitter saliva. This didn't make sense. Steve was interested in her. But why didn't they ever go out on Saturday night? Did he have another girlfriend—one that he reserved for Saturday nights? Was Pam only his Friday-night fling?

She bit her lip, then put on her turn signal and stopped at the corner. Tears pooled in her eyes.

Stop it, she told herself. *Don't jump to conclusions.*

Maybe Steve was with his mother—or his sister, Carol. Pam had to find out.

She checked her rearview mirror. Steve's car was still visible on Main Street. There was no traffic near her. She whipped into a U-Turn and sped up to catch him.

At the end of the block, he paused before turning right on red, giving her time to get closer. The streetlight at the corner gave her a clear view of the person in the passenger seat. She recognized the teased hair and over-done makeup, even at this distance.

Susan Wilbanks was riding with Steve—on Saturday night.

Pam watched as Susan threw her head back and laughed—undoubtedly at something amusing that Steve had said—and turned to look into the back seat. Pam didn't see who Susan was talking to.

The traffic light turned green, and she drove slowly through the intersection. The tears that had been pooling under her eyes now ran down her cheeks. She pulled to the curb and put her car in park, resting her forehead against the steering wheel.

How in the world had she been so stupid—to trust a man, again? Steve and his "no dating" pledge. She'd believed everything he'd said about relationships and integrity; finding the right person and being happy alone until he did. She'd bought it all. She swept her tears from her damp cheeks. He'd probably been seeing Susan the whole time. Hadn't there been talk at the gym that Susan's husband had filed for divorce because she'd been unfaithful? No one had guessed the other man was Steve.

Pam pounded the steering wheel with her fist. This was the last straw. She was done with Steve; done with men.

The fatigue of the past week, amplified by the emotional turmoil brought on by seeing Steve with Susan, threatened to drown her.

Pam started her car and drove slowly home. The only thing she wanted to do now was feed Leopold, take a shower, and fall into bed.

THE RHYTHMIC PRESSURE of Leopold's paws on her chest woke Pam the next morning. She opened one eye, then closed it quickly. Her bedroom was bathed in sunlight that penetrated the cracks in her curtains.

"Okay—that's enough," she said as she pushed her cat, who was insisting that it was time for his breakfast, to one side. Pam swung her feet to the floor and checked the time on her bedside clock. It was almost eleven.

The shock that she had slept the morning away brought her fully awake. She'd gone straight to bed after her shower the night before, but had tossed and turned, revisiting the images of Steve and Susan. The last time she remembered looking at the time it was five o'clock.

Pam hurried to the kitchen, fed Leopold, and started brewing a cup of coffee. She returned to her bedroom, put on the clothes she'd worn the day before, and picked up her coffee on the way out the door. If she was going to complete the work on her mother's bathroom that she'd scheduled for this weekend, she needed to get going.

Irene sat in a wicker chair on her front porch, her feet on an ottoman, with the Sunday paper spread around her. She looked over the top of the *Leisure and Lifestyle* section as Pam took the steps to the porch, two at a time.

"Good morning, dear," Irene said. "I'm so glad you slept in."

Pam nodded at her mother. She left her sunglasses on. If Irene saw her puffy eyes, she'd know something was wrong. Pam didn't have the energy to relive it all right now.

"I'd better get busy," she said and kept moving.

"There's a nice article in here about your new show: *Wishes of Home*. They even mention you as the host! I'll save this for you," Irene called after Pam, folding the newspaper section and setting it aside.

Pam tackled the remaining cleanup and preparation work with a vengeance, blocking out the unwanted images that attempted to submerge her thoughts. The manual labor commanded all her attention and she gave herself over to it. At four forty-five, she dumped the last bucket of debris into the dumpster tucked up against the garage.

Pam washed her hands at the kitchen sink, then went in search of her mother.

Irene was in her sewing room, hunched over her faithful Singer. The machine hummed at high speed as she expertly fed fabric under the presser foot.

Pam waited until Irene finished the seam she was working on. "I'm done, so I think I'll get going."

Irene clipped the threads on the table runner and set it aside. "What time is it?"

Pam told her.

"That late? You were fully occupied in there and I didn't want to disturb you, so I got busy in here. I guess we both lost track of time. I meant to start dinner earlier." She looked apologetic. "Would you like to grab an early dinner?"

Pam shook her head. "I think I'll head home."

Irene rose. "Let me give you that newspaper article." She led the way to the console table inside her front door and handed Pam the paper. "I'm so proud of you, dear."

Pam took it and turned aside, avoiding Irene's eyes.

Irene stepped around her and put her hands on Pam's shoulders. "I'm concerned. You look exhausted."

Pam stared at her feet.

"You also look sad. Really sad." Irene waited.

Pam didn't respond.

"Something's happened, hasn't it?"

Pam swallowed hard.

"It's Steve, isn't it? This stupid bathroom is taking up too much of your time."

"It's Steve, but your bathroom has nothing to do with

it." Pam fought against the tears threatening to breach the barrier she'd maintained against them all afternoon.

Irene moved her hand down to Pam's arm. "Oh, sweetie…"

"I'm not… I can't talk about him right now, Mom. I'm sorry, but I just can't."

"I understand. I'm here whenever you're ready," Irene said.

Pam hugged her mother briefly before fleeing out the front door.

"Remember," Irene said.

Pam stopped at the top step, her back to her mother.

"Things often aren't what they seem."

Perhaps not, but Pam saw what she saw and it was clear.

She nodded to her mother but didn't turn around as she continued to her car, climbed in and drove off.

CHAPTER 15

Steve caught up with Pam as she sped past the sign-in desk at Linden Falls Fitness and headed for the entrance. "Hey," he said, intercepting her as she reached for the metal bar that would open the door, "I haven't seen you all week."

Pam stopped and turned to him, her hand still on the door.

"You haven't responded to any of my texts." He noted the dark circles under her eyes. "Are you working yourself to death on this TV show?"

"It's not that." Her voice was flat.

"Well—what is it then? If it's not the show, that means you're purposely ghosting me." He drew himself back. "Are you mad at me?"

A group of women from the yoga class that had just concluded surged toward the doors, separating them.

Steve took Pam's arm and pulled her aside.

"I don't want to talk about it now and especially not here." She wriggled out of his grasp.

"Friday night?"

"No. I can't."

Steve took a step back and stared at her.

Pam turned away and joined the women exiting the building.

Steve followed her to her car.

"What's wrong with you? I can't believe this is happening. Please, tell me what I've done."

Pam opened her car door.

Steve pushed it shut. He looked devastated. "You at least owe me an explanation."

She looked at him; saw the hurt in his eyes. He looked genuinely perplexed.

Steve stepped closer. "Pam—it's me! What is it?"

Her heart did the flip-flop it always did when he was near. Even now—when she knew she was only his Friday night woman. She looked up at him and felt her resolve weaken.

He cupped her cheek with one hand.

She turned her head aside as the memory of Susan's face in his car flooded her mind. "I'm late for filming. I've got to go."

Steve dropped his hand.

She could see she'd wounded him and she took no pleasure in it. "I'm just tired and busy," she lied.

"You'll call when you're ready to talk?"

Pam nodded, then got into her car and drove away.

JED HAILED Steve as he walked in the back door of Duncan's Hardware.

Steve joined his friend. "I'm here to pick up those banners."

"I've got them in my office. Follow me."

"I really appreciate Duncan's sponsorship of the soccer tournament. You've always been more than generous."

The two men walked to Jed's office at the back of the store. Small but neat, the office was furnished with a worn wooden desk pushed against the wall underneath a window overlooking the parking lot. A computer and keyboard sat on the desk, together with a set of stacking trays that corralled the reports and papers that Jed relied on. Jed's tall mug of coffee, which had long ago grown cold, sat on a coaster. A wobbly looking desk chair on casters and a straight-backed guest chair completed the decor.

Jed sat and motioned Steve into the guest chair. He tapped a group of six cardboard cylinders leaning against the side of the desk. "They're all in here. You needed six of them, right?"

"Yep. We'll hang one over the entrance to the soccer fields, one at the concession stand, and the others will go on the fences around the fields."

"That'll work."

"Will you come to the tournament?" Steve tilted back in his chair, the front two legs coming off the floor.

"I'm planning on it."

"I was thinking you could open the tournament."

"Sure." Jed ran his tongue over his upper teeth. "I was wondering about something. The tournament starts the same day that the first episode of *Wishes of Home* airs. Would it be all right with you if Pam and I opened the tournament and said something about the show?"

"Of course. That's a great idea." Steve brought the front of his chair back to the floor and rested his elbows on his knees. "Except I'm not sure Pam will come."

"What're you talking about?"

"Something's wrong between us." He sucked in a deep breath. "I think she's breaking up with me."

"Is that what she said?"

"Not in so many words. She's avoiding me. I tried to talk to her earlier, and she said that she was busy and tired. That she'd talk to me later."

"I think that's all this is. Hosting this show—on her own—is proving to be too much for her."

"You really think so?"

"Yes. In fact, she was just in here picking up fittings for tonight's filming and she bit the head off the cashier."

"That doesn't sound like Pam. She doesn't say a cross word to anybody."

"I know. We were all shocked. I think the stress is getting to her." He looked at Steve. "You really like her, don't you?"

Steve nodded. "I do. I've been all torn up over how she's been acting lately."

"It's not you, I'm sure of it."

"Maybe not." Steve got to his feet and gathered up the cylinders containing the promotional banners.

"Count on it," Jed said, walking Steve out of his office.

They were almost at the back door when Marty entered.

"Just the man I'm looking for," Marty greeted Jed. "When you have a moment."

"Let me introduce the two of you," Jed said, doing the honors.

Marty and Steve shook hands.

"I'm looking forward to this new show of yours," Steve said. "It's the talk of the town."

"It's going to be great," Marty said. "We have a few wrinkles to sort out—which is why I'm here to see Jed—but we'll get them handled. I think *Wishes of Home* is going to be a very successful—and profitable—venture for Duncan's Hardware."

"I'll leave you to it," Steve said. "I've got to get going. Nice to meet you, Marty."

"You, as well," Marty said as Steve pushed through the door.

"WHAT CAN I DO TO HELP?" Jed turned to Marty as soon as Steve left. "Do you need me to send over another worker to help Pam?"

"Can we discuss this somewhere private?"

"It's that bad? Follow me." Jed led Marty to his office and closed the door behind them. Jed took his seat again.

Marty paced. "Pam's design ideas are terrific and she knows what she's doing when she's doing the actual work —or directing others to do it—but she's a completely different person when she's on camera by herself."

"I thought you said she'd get the hang of it—that it takes time."

Marty raked his fingers through his hair. "That's what I said, but she's getting worse rather than better. I went through last night's footage this morning. It's a disaster."

"Isn't that what editing is for?"

"We can't correct all of this with editing." He stopped

pacing and looked at Jed. "I know how much this TV show means to you. We need to hit it out of the park on these first episodes. So far that's not happening."

Jed pulled his hand across his chin. "We've got to fix this. What can we do?"

"We talked about bringing in a co-host. We'll keep Pam involved for this project and see if she improves. Maybe bantering on air with someone else is all she'll need. If she doesn't improve, we can replace her for any future projects."

"If that's what you think is necessary. She's a great person and has been very supportive of Duncan's. I don't want to dump her. This is a close-knit small town—people won't like that." He looked at his hands. "I won't like it. We're all very fond of Pam around here."

"Remember, Jed, your viewership won't be limited to Linden Falls. One of your goals for this show is to increase your market share across the state."

"That's right."

"I'd like to bring someone in as soon as possible. We'll reshoot segments from the very beginning so that the series is cohesive from the get-go. That way, it won't look like you're making a change early on in the show."

"You can do that?"

"We think so. We'd only need to redo the parts where Pam is on-screen by herself, explaining things."

"Good. That would be best."

"Now all we need to do is find our new co-host." Marty cleared his throat. "We don't have much time. Would you do it?"

Jed shook his head. He got out of his chair and joined

Marty at the window. "I have a suggestion for you. He's someone who I think will be ideal."

Marty raised an eyebrow.

"Remember that man I introduced you to when you came in today?"

"The tall guy? Looks like he works out?"

"That's the one. He'd be perfect—and I'm sure he'd do it."

Marty looked at his watch. "I need to get over to Irene's house for tonight's filming. Walk me to my car and tell me why you think so."

Jed talked as he and Marty walked. By the time they got to Marty's car, both men were smiling.

"I'll call Steve first thing in the morning," Marty said. "If they're as good together as you say they are, this is exactly what we need."

CHAPTER 16

*P*am stood in the shadows on Irene's front porch, waiting for Marty to finish his conversation with the cameraman. "We can go over what you've got in the morning. See you at the studio," Marty said.

The camera man joined the rest of the crew who were packing up their gear. They'd finished the week's shooting. It was almost eleven.

Marty headed for the steps.

Pam called to him.

He turned to her, fatigue etched in his face.

"I know you're tired. I won't keep you." She glanced nervously around herself. "I just want to say... I know that..." She wrung her hands. "I'm terrible in front of the camera by myself—and getting worse, not better. Surely you can see that."

Some of the lines around his eyes eased. He nodded in agreement.

"What're we going to do? I even bought a whole bunch

of books about public speaking—by Dale Carnegie and others. None of them helped. I don't want this show to fail because of me. Jed deserves better."

"I've been thinking," Marty continued slowly, gauging her reaction, "what would you say to our bringing in a co-host?"

"How would that work?"

"Instead of making speeches to a camera, you'd be having a conversation with someone else. It'd feel much more natural to you."

Her shoulders relaxed. "That's a great idea. But do you have time to find someone—isn't it too late for that?"

"No. I've talked to Jed and he had some suggestions. We can re-film the segments from these first two weeks where you're on-screen by yourself. We'll bring in the new co-host so everything is seamless from the beginning."

"Really? Won't it look strange?"

"Not at all. We'll work our magic in editing."

A smile played at the corner of Pam's lips for the first time since they'd started filming the show. "I'm so relieved. I haven't been sleeping. All I can think about is how nervous I am on-screen."

Marty put his hand on her shoulder. "Stop worrying—as of right now. Do you have anyone you'd like to suggest as your co-host?"

Pam covered her mouth to hide a big yawn. "I'll be fine with anyone you pick." She yawned again. "Sorry about that. Now that I know there's a solution in sight, all I want to do is go home and get some sleep."

"You do that," he replied, ushering them both down the steps. "Leave everything to me."

Pam nodded and headed toward her car.

"Pam," he called after her. "Can you leave your schedule open next Tuesday and Friday? That's when I'd like to re-film those segments."

Pam raised her hand over her head and gave him the thumbs-up sign as she continued on her way.

PAM CHECKED the clock on the wall above the reception desk at Linden Falls Fitness. At four-fifteen, Steve would be working with a client. Pam was usually busy then, too, but her final two clients of the day had canceled. She was thankful. She wanted nothing more than to go home, eat the rest of the salad leftover from her lunch, and take a long soak in her tub.

This would be a Friday night she wasn't spending with Steve. The memory of their romantic dinner at Bistro Claudine flooded her thoughts and hot tears welled up. She swallowed hard, pushing them back. She'd been wrong about Steve and was better off knowing that unfortunate fact sooner rather than later.

If she had her way, she'd never talk to him again. That they both worked at the gym complicated things. She'd avoided him all week and would continue to do so. Knowing his schedule helped.

Pam hurried to the stairs and raced up to the second floor. She'd get her purse and jacket from her locker in the trainer's break room and be out the door before he finished with his client.

Pam yanked open the door to the break room and found herself face-to-face with Steve.

They stared at each other. Each of them appeared to be searching for words.

"I thought you had a client," Pam blurted out.

"I usually do. We rescheduled. I'm on my way to get cleaned up for a dinner meeting." He searched her face. "You told me you wouldn't be able to go out tonight."

"That's right." Pam stepped aside. "Don't let me keep you."

"Helping Irene at the market in the morning?"

"Mom's not setting up her booth tomorrow. It's pouring out there now and is supposed to continue all weekend. I'll be working on her bathroom remodel."

"The whole weekend?" He leaned ever so slightly toward her.

Pam felt herself flush at the nearness of him. She raised her eyes to his and felt her resolve weaken.

"I could stop by after my dinner. I'll pick up some ice cream and we can watch a sappy movie."

Pam took a step back. Here he was—offering her a few hours on Friday night. Again. Probably saving Saturday night for Susan Wilbanks. "No. I don't have time. I've got things to work on for the show."

Steve recoiled at her brisk tone. "See you around next week," he said and headed toward the stairs.

Pam entered the break room, forcing herself to not slam the door firmly behind her. How could Steve seem like such a genuinely nice, sincere guy? He'd fooled her for a long time, but at least now she knew better.

She rested her forehead against the cool metal door of her locker and took deep breaths to calm her racing emotions. She'd be darned if she was going to spend another sleepless night crying over Steve Turner.

Pam waited another five minutes to allow Steve plenty of time to have left the parking lot, then went to her car and made the lonely drive home.

CHAPTER 17

*N*eva Cabot was manning the hostess station of the dining room at the Wishing Tree Inn. Breeze was usually the hostess, but she had a big exam to study for and Neva had insisted she focus on that for the next few days.

Thankfully, with the continuing heavy rain from the past few days, reservations were light on this Friday night and Neva could easily handle the dining room duties on her own.

The front door to the inn opened on a gust of wind and rain that carried to the hostess stand as Steve stepped inside.

"Hello, you." Neva greeted the man she liked so well, smiling at the memory of the Valentine's Day blind date in that very dining room where he and Pam had finally gotten together. "Are you meeting Pam?"

Steve's expression dimmed. "Not tonight."

Neva tilted her head to one side. "Everything all right between the two of you?"

"If you'd have asked me that a week ago, I would have said yes. Now? I'm not sure."

"What's happened?"

"I honestly don't know."

Neva drew a deep breath. "Have you asked her?"

"I've tried. She won't tell me what's wrong."

"I saw Irene this morning. She said this new show is taking its toll on Pam. She's working herself to death."

"That's what Pam implied."

"There." Neva brightened. "See? She's just overworked. The best thing you can do is give her the space to get through this. And if you find a way to help her, do it."

"You really think so?"

"Yes." She patted his arm. "All relationships go through ups and downs. You'll get past this."

"I sure hope you're right. I'm crazy about her, but this last week? Maybe I'm wrong about her."

"I still believe the two of you are terrific for each other." She pointed toward the town square behind him. "The Wishing Tree granted your wish to be together, remember?"

Steve held up a hand, laughing. "Don't start with that Wishing Tree stuff, Neva. I know you believe it, but I don't."

Neva tsked at him. "Believe what you like. I know it's true." She smiled at him and picked up a menu. "Table for one?"

"No. I'm meeting…"

The door behind him opened, and Marty surged over the threshold, pushed by the wind.

"Marty," Steve said, stepping around him to force the door shut.

111

"What a night!" Marty said as the two men shook hands.

"Let me show you to your table," Neva said. "I've got a nice spot by the fireplace for you and you are going to love what Carly has cooked up for the evening special."

The two men settled into the comfortable spot and ordered beverages.

"Thanks for meeting me on such short notice," Marty said.

Steve nodded. "I have to admit—I'm intrigued. What can I do to help you?"

The server brought their drinks and set a tray of crudites with a dish of spicy hummus in the center of the table.

"Jed tells me you're close to Pam Olson." He peered at Steve over the top of his glass.

Steve nodded.

"Has she told you anything about these first two weeks of filming?"

"We haven't talked about it this week, but she was pretty freaked out about it last week. She felt she was horrible." Steve shook his head. "I told her she couldn't have been as bad as all that. She must have been..." He stopped short as Marty's mouth settled into a thin line.

"Was she really that bad?"

"Terrible. Deer in the headlights. Even after editing, it's uncomfortable to watch."

"I can't imagine that. The local television station inter-viewed us about the toy drive and we were terrific. Everyone raved about what a natural Pam was in front of a camera."

"That's what we'd hoped for," Marty said. "In hindsight, I think Pam's fabulous when she's with someone else, but she's not a solo act."

Steve frowned. "I'm sorry to hear that. I thought she was exaggerating."

Marty shook his head slowly.

"No wonder she's been so…"

"Snippy?"

"I thought she was mad at me."

"She's frustrated, scared, and upset," Marty said. "The longer this goes on, the worse she does. We're in a vicious cycle."

Steve raked his hand through his hair. "Poor Pam. I hate hearing this. I wish she would have told me."

"Don't blame her. I kept telling her she'd improve. Which she hasn't."

The server approached and asked if they had any questions on the menu. She announced the special for the night.

"Yes! New York strip is my favorite. Is it good here?" Marty asked.

"Terrific, sir. We serve it with roasted fingerling potatoes and haricot verts."

Marty raised his eyebrows at Steve in a silent question.

"Yep, I'll have that," Steve confirmed. "Rare."

"Make that two," Marty said, handing the server his menu.

"She's very committed to making *Wishes of Home* a success for Jed," Steve said, picking the conversation back up. "She'd hate to be the reason it failed."

"Which brings me to why I asked you to have dinner with me." Marty leaned forward in his chair. "We can't continue as we are."

"You're not thinking of replacing Pam, are you?" He pushed against his seat back. "You can't fire her!"

Marty held his hands up to calm Steve. "Hold up. We're not planning anything of the kind. I've viewed this toy drive segment you mentioned. The two of you are great together—natural and charismatic. We thought Pam would bring those same qualities to the screen on her own, but that segment was so successful because of the chemistry the two of you have together."

Steve stared at Marty, confused at what he was getting to.

"We made the mistake of breaking up a duet—a mistake we'd like to rectify." Marty leaned further across the table. "I'm here to offer you a position as co-host of *Wishes of Home*."

Steve's jaw dropped. "Me? A co-host of a home improvement show?"

"Jed told me you're handy around the house. You know what you're doing."

"That may be true, but I don't have any design sense whatsoever."

"Pam's got that covered. Your function will be to introduce topics by discussing them on camera with Pam. You see this format all over HGTV. It works—and people love watching couples."

Steve narrowed his eyes. "Have you told Pam she won't be doing it solo anymore?"

"We talked about it and I've decided to go with a co-host, no matter what. The show requires it and Pam was open to it, too. Jed suggested you."

"So, I'll just be talking with Pam on camera?"

"We'll also film you doing some of the remodeling work, if that's okay with you."

Steve shifted in his seat.

"You'd be helping Jed. And Pam."

Steve turned his face aside, then spoke. "If I can help Jed and Pam, I'm happy to do it. I'm a personal trainer—just like Pam—so I'm assuming my hours would be the same as what she's doing now?"

"That's right. We're prepared to pay you very well for stepping in…"

"More than you're paying Pam?" Steve interrupted.

"Yes. Under the circumstances…" Marty looked at Steve and stopped talking.

"I'm not doing this for the money," Steve said. "I'm sure Jed is footing the bill. Pay me what you pay Pam."

"That's a very principled thing to do," Marty said.

Steve shrugged.

The server brought their steaks and placed them on the table, together with two large, serrated knives. "Please let me know if you need anything else," she said before leaving them to their conversation.

"As for our schedule, we'd like to work two extra days this week to re-film segments already in the can." Marty picked up his knife and sliced into the fragrant steak. "That means we'll be on set Tuesday through Friday, from three until ten."

"I can make that work," Steve said.

"Fabulous. When *Wishes of Home* airs, you'll be there from the very beginning. No one will ever know about the rocky start."

"Good, but I won't do this if it will upset or embarrass Pam."

"I think it'll be a relief to her to not carry the show alone any more."

"I never thought you'd be offering me a job tonight," Steve said, his eyes wide. He picked up his fork and tucked into his meal. "You'd better fill me in on anything I need to know before Tuesday."

"I'll tell you everything while we eat. But there's one more thing. Can you stop by the studio tomorrow morning to meet with makeup and wardrobe?"

"Sure."

"Thanks, Steve, for accepting this last-minute offer. You won't be sorry. With your addition to the cast, *Wishes of Home* is going to be a tremendous success."

CHAPTER 18

*P*am hurried to her car on Tuesday afternoon. Her final client had been extra chatty and Pam had spent an extra ten minutes with her to finish her workout.

Marty had texted Pam over the weekend to tell her he'd found a co-host and asked her to report to Irene's on Tuesday to begin re-filming. Pam would be late arriving at her mom's house and she hated not being punctual.

As she quickly walked to the parking lot, Pam glanced toward the spot where Steve usually parked and was surprised that it was vacant.

She scanned the lot.

His SUV wasn't there. She wondered idly where he could be—their schedules were usually packed during the late afternoon and just-after-work hours. She hoped he wasn't sick. They weren't going to be an item any longer, but that didn't mean she couldn't be concerned.

She clicked her SUV open with her key fob and slid

behind the wheel, then checked her reflection in the rearview mirror.

The bags under her eyes stood as testament to the long hours she'd put in over the weekend, installing the rest of the tile.

She removed the elastic band that corralled her ponytail, allowing her thick chestnut mane to caress her shoulders. A swipe of lip gloss completed her efforts. She was thankful that the stylists would attend to her hair and makeup before she went on camera.

The ride was uneventful and Pam parked at the curb two houses down from her mother's house. She knew, by now, that the vehicles required for filming would occupy all the closer spots.

She put her head down and raced to the house, ignoring the increasing level of activity as she drew close. Pam didn't notice the familiar SUV parked on the other side of the street.

Irene stood on the porch and greeted her daughter. "They're waiting for you—by the bathroom."

"I know I'm late," Pam said.

Irene held out a hand and took Pam's purse from her. She narrowed her eyes at her daughter. "What do you think about your co-host?"

"Oh, I haven't met him—or her—yet." She continued on her way and didn't see her mother's eyebrows shoot up.

Pam walked into the hallway and came to an abrupt halt. Marty was standing at the end, talking to a man who had his back to her. The makeup artist was dabbing at the man's forehead with a cotton ball.

It was a very familiar forehead.

Pam knew, even before they all turned to her, that the co-host was Steve Turner.

She took a step back. The space suddenly seemed unbearably warm. Her hair clung to the back of her neck.

Steve flashed her his full-on smile. The one that still made her knees weak and her heart turn over.

"Looks like we'll be together on-screen, again," he said.

Pam took a deep breath and forced herself to move toward him.

"I would've called you to talk it over, but I thought I'd surprise you with our new, perfectly matched, co-host," Marty said in a voice that was a bit too loud.

Pam gave them all a thin smile.

"Why don't you go with these folks," he pointed to the two stylists, "while we finish explaining our setup to Steve."

Pam nodded, glad for the opportunity to step away and gather herself. She was sure her eyes were bulging. Steve was going to be her co-host—and obviously, it was a done deal. She'd have to be professional and somehow make peace with Steve—at least on camera and until they finished filming in the next couple of months.

Pam bit her lip to stop it from quivering. She had to see Steve at the gym every workday, and now this. It seemed like the universe was conspiring to throw them together.

She didn't like it one little bit.

The stylist began work on her hair. The makeup artist asked her to unclench her teeth. Pam forced herself to concentrate on their instructions. Actresses worked with former spouses or cheating boyfriends all the time.

If they could do it, so could she.

Ten minutes later, Pam and Steve were standing outside the door to the bathroom.

"Face the camera," Marty said.

They did as they were instructed.

"Stand closer together," the cameraman said, motioning Steve next to Pam until their shoulders touched. "That's good," the man said. "We're in such tight quarters that you'll need to stay close."

"No problem for me," Steve said softly to Pam.

She felt an involuntary quiver and tried to put a bit more room between them without being obvious.

"We're going to start with the very first segment, where you'll introduce the project," Marty said. "Steve— you'll give an overview, then turn to Pam and start asking the questions on your script."

"I haven't seen the script," Pam said, a note of alarm in her voice.

"We thought it would be better if you don't," Marty said. "You're just going to be talking to Steve. It'll seem more natural that way."

Pam glanced at Steve, and he smiled at her. "We're going to hit it out of the park. You'll see."

She forced herself not to return his smile.

The assistant snapped the clapperboard, and Steve began talking to the camera. His introduction was conversational; his natural charm evident.

The first question to Pam was about the goals of the remodel and she loosened up.

Marty's shoulders relaxed.

They continued filming until almost ten.

"Good work, everyone," Marty said. He addressed Pam and Steve. "You were terrific together. Viewers are going to love you. This is exactly what the show needs." He took a step back. "Jed's got workers scheduled to help us tomorrow and Thursday, so we'll continue with our existing plans for those nights. We'll finish up the rest of the segments that need to be redone on Friday night."

"Looks like we'll be together this Friday night after all," Steve leaned close and whispered in Pam's ear.

His warm breath sent a shiver down her spine. "Maybe we can grab dinner when we're done."

She pulled back, fighting the urge to tell him she'd never have dinner with him again. This was not the time or place to have that discussion. She needed to hold her emotions in check until they finished filming this series.

She owed that much to Jed.

"I've got to go," she said as her mother appeared at the end of the hallway. Pam joined her. They disappeared into the kitchen, leaving Steve to stare after them before making his way with the others out the front door.

"That went great. The two of you have such an easy, playful way together." Irene glanced at her daughter, then stepped close and looked into her face. "You're crying."

Pam nodded, swiping at the tears on her cheeks.

"What's wrong? Something's been bothering you for weeks."

Pam looked away.

"Why won't you tell me? You've always talked to me about your problems."

Pam remained silent.

"It's about Steve, isn't it?"

Pam drew a shaky breath. "I can't... not right now. I need to get through *Wishes of Home* and then I'll be ready to talk."

Irene reached for her daughter and pulled her into a hug. "If that's what you need. Just remember, I'm here for you. Sometimes it helps to talk. Maybe things aren't as bad as you think they are."

Pam stiffened.

Irene continued to hold her. "I'm always on your side," she said before releasing her daughter.

"I know, Mom." Pam kissed her mother's cheek. "See you tomorrow. I'm heading home. We both need to get some sleep."

JED JOINED Marty and Irene on her front porch. "The tile work on the shower is fabulous," he said. "I'm going to get Pam to consult with me on my master bath."

Irene's smile widened. "I'm so proud of her. That rainfall shower head arrangement is fantastic. I can't believe I'm going to have something so nice. Thank you for supplying all the materials."

"I'm the one who should thank you," Jed said. "Marty tells me you've been kind to everyone and very patient with this process. Your home is a mad house whenever they're here filming." He looked at her. "Seriously—it must get old."

"I'm thrilled to be helping Pam and I'm getting a new bathroom. That's a win-win for me." She spoke to Marty. "Pam tells me you're pleased with the co-host arrangement."

"It's going great—even better than I'd hoped."

"The first episode airs a week from Saturday. Will you be ready?" Jed asked.

"Absolutely. The first two episodes are in final editing. The segments we re-filmed turned out great. We've decided to film some additional promotional spots this Tuesday evening, and then we'll be back to our Wednesday and Thursday evening shooting schedule."

"That's a relief to hear. I was worried for a while there." Jed glanced at Irene and cleared his throat. "It's going to be a big day of promotions at Duncan's that day. We're going to include the products featured in that week's show in our weekly sale. There will be donuts and coffee all morning and we'll show *Wishes of Home* on a couple of wide-screen televisions we're having installed tomorrow. We'll record it and show it on a loop."

"I'm so glad to hear this! I'll send Pam over to watch it live. She insists that she's going to help me with my booth at the market that morning. I'd cancel my booth, but it's supposed to be a nice day and I've been rained out too many Saturdays this spring."

"Maybe you and Pam can take turns coming to Duncan's to watch," Jed said. "After all, your bathroom," he gestured to the house behind him with his thumb, "is one of the stars of the show."

Irene clapped her hands together. "This is going to be so much fun! I'll put up a sign at my booth, too."

Marty nodded to the man walking up the driveway. An elaborate camera hung from a thick strap over his shoulder. "We'll have our photographer take some publicity photos with the three of us," Marty said. "You can both use them."

"Great idea," Jed said. "I'll post them on social media, too."

"My hair's a mess," Irene said, reaching up to comb it with her fingers. "And I need to touch up my makeup."

"Nonsense," Jed said. "You look terrific. Your beautiful daughter obviously got her looks from her mother."

Irene flushed.

"This will be excellent," the photographer said as he walked up the steps to join them. "The light this morning —with the high cloud cover—is ideal. If I can have the three of you take a giant step to the left…"

CHAPTER 19

*I*rene caught Pam's eye on the other side of the booth, where Pam was helping a customer find coordinating napkins for the placements the woman had selected. Irene tapped the watch on her left wrist in an exaggerated fashion and motioned with her head for Pam to be on her way. It was nine o'clock and the first episode of *Wishes of Home* aired at ten.

Pam nodded. She spoke to her customer and pointed to her mother before slipping around the display table and walking out of the booth.

Irene waved to the customer. She was about to walk over to her when Irene heard her name being called. She turned and found Neva striding into the booth.

"I just passed Pam," Neva said. "She said she's on her way to Jed's—that the hair and makeup artists from the show are going to touch her up for the premiere."

"It's so exciting, isn't it?" Irene asked. "I'm recording it and I can't wait to get home to watch."

"You won't have to wait until you get home," Neva

replied. "I'm going to man your booth for you so you can watch the premiere with your daughter."

"That's so nice, but I can't let you do that!"

"You can and you will," Neva said, taking Irene by the shoulders and steering her to the front of the booth. "I know your merchandise almost as well as you do." She held up her cell phone. "And if I have questions, I'll call you."

Irene hesitated, a smile spreading across her lips.

"You should be there, dear," Neva told her friend. "Don't worry about anything here. I've got it."

Irene leaned in and gave Neva a hug. "Thank you so much. I want to see it with Pam."

"Then go!"

Irene laughed and hurried across the square toward Duncan's Hardware. By the time she got there, the place was buzzing with activity. A balloon arch over the entrance from the square announced the premiere of *Wishes of Home*. Life-sized cutouts of Pam and Steve stood on either side of the door. A banner invited everyone to come inside. Jed's sister, Paige, directed people to the back parking lot for free donuts and coffee. Gladys hovered near the food, greeting everyone with her golden retriever friendliness while hoping that someone would slip her a donut.

Irene weaved her way through the crowded store, passing Calvin and Courtney, who appeared excited and prepared to do a story for the town newspaper. He looked at his watch and began to shuffle Courtney toward the back, falling in behind Irene.

Television sets were mounted from the ceiling and

played the promotional trailers for the series. Employees handed out raffle tickets.

Irene stepped out the back door where a sizable portion of the parking area had been roped off.

A tent covered most of the space. The largest television set she'd ever seen, flanked by tall speakers on either side, sat on top of a flatbed trailer at the far end of the tent. A maze of cords snaked their way inside the store. Chairs for fifty people were arranged in neat rows in front of the television and she saw that Janie and Max and their two girls had already claimed four of them, and Henry Harmon took a fifth beside Carly.

Irene shielded her eyes from the sun with her hand and searched for Pam. She found her off to one side. The makeup artist was patting her face with a large powder puff while Pam made a face like she was sucking a lemon.

Her daughter had never liked to get fancied up and Irene stifled a giggle.

She saw Steve standing to the side with Jed and Marty, then watched as Steve said something and both men threw back their heads and laughed.

Unlike Pam, Steve looked completely at ease and she did so love a confident man.

Irene made her way to the coffee station and waited in line for a cup before selecting a seat on the aisle in the second row. The first row was roped off with a sign that read "reserved."

A microphone crackled, followed by Jed's voice. "Good morning, everyone. Thank you for turning out for this premier of *Wishes of Home*, proudly sponsored by Duncan's Hardware. The show's going to start soon, so please take a seat under the tent."

He gestured to Marty and Steve to join him as he walked to the front row. He stopped when he came upon Irene. "I'm glad you're here. It wouldn't feel right without you."

"I've got Neva to thank for that. She's covering for me at the market."

"If someone needs help, you can always count on Neva." Jed took Irene's elbow and pulled her to her feet. "You're going to sit up here, with us." He steered her to a chair in the front row. "Right next to your celebrity daughter."

Irene squeezed his hand as Pam joined her, raising an eyebrow quizzically.

"Neva," they both said in unison and laughed.

Steve took his seat on the other side of Pam.

Jed stepped back to the microphone and resumed his remarks. "We know you're going to love our hosts— Linden Falls' very own Pam Olson and Steve Turner." He motioned for them to stand and turn to wave at the people seated behind them.

A smattering of applause greeted them.

"I want to thank our director, Marty Beckman," Jed pointed to Marty, who raised his hand in acknowledgment, "and the rest of the crew who made this production possible. And now—as they say—sit back and enjoy the show!"

Jed took his seat as the opening sequence appeared on the screen. Footage of the town square, lingering on the front of Duncan's Hardware, segued into shots of picket fences, window boxes, hanging baskets, and wide front porches. Names appeared on the screen, with the final two appearing in a large font in front of the iconic linden tree known as the Wishing Tree: *With your Co-Hosts, Pam Olson and Steve Turner.*

Irene sniffled and rummaged in her purse for a tissue.

Steve grabbed Pam's hand and held it.

The scene shifted into the introduction of the project, with Pam and Steve talking to Irene about her outdated master bathroom.

Pam pulled her hand out of Steve's and placed it in her lap, out of his reach.

Steve stiffened in his seat and leaned away from her.

The thirty-minute segment rolled to its conclusion. The people in the chairs and those standing around the periphery clapped, whistled, and cheered.

Irene threw her arms around Pam in an enthusiastic hug.

Several of the onlookers surged Jed, shaking his hand, clapping him on the back, and congratulating him.

Paige caught her brother's eye and gave him the thumbs-up sign with both hands.

Steve got to his feet and turned to Pam.

She looked away.

He exited the row, congratulated Jed and Marty on the successful launch of *Wishes of Home*, and walked out of the hardware store.

Irene looked at her daughter. "Something's wrong. Go after him, honey."

"Mom," Pam practically hissed. "Stop."

Irene saw that Pam was fighting back tears.

"I'm going to say goodbye to Jed and Marty and get out of here, too. Do you mind if I don't go back to the market? I want to head home."

"That's fine, honey. I can handle it on my own. It's

almost over for the day, anyway." Irene got up. "Call me if you want to talk."

Pam nodded and went to Jed. He scooped her into a hug before she could utter a word. "You were fabulous," Jed said. He looked over the top of Pam's head at Marty. "Bringing in Steve as a co-host was a genius idea. I think it really worked."

Marty grinned. "Like a charm. Pam—you were articulate and engaging. I'm so proud of you. I know I directed it, but this is good television. You can see by their reaction," he gestured to the people around them, "that *Wishes of Home* will be a huge success."

"Thank you, Pam, for hanging in there and for doing the actual remodeling work," Jed said.

"You're welcome. It's my happy place."

"You could start a business as a designer. I'm sure some of these people would love to talk to you." He looked at the people milling about.

"Actually, I'm headed home. I'm beat—and I'm getting a headache."

"Okay. Rest up and feel better. We'll still see you at the tournament tonight?"

Pam cocked her head to one side. "What're you talking about?"

"The soccer tournament tonight. Duncan's is sponsoring it. The three of us are going to open play." Jed bit his lower lip. "Did I forget to mention this to you?"

She nodded.

"I'm so sorry. Can you make it?"

She drew in a deep breath. "Sure. Where is this?"

Jed gave her the address. "It's an evening league. Can you be there at four-thirty?"

"Sure. The third person is…?"

"Steve."

"He's going to be there?"

"Well… of course." Jed gave her a quizzical look.

"I'll see you later, then."

"Thanks, Pam. I appreciate your making time for this at the last minute."

"Always happy to help."

CHAPTER 20

*P*am arrived at the soccer fields at four-twenty. The lot was full. Steve's SUV was parked in the front row. She weaved her way through the surrounding streets until she found a spot along the curb. She grabbed her purse and jogged back to the low, one-story building that sat at the entrance to the fields. It was four thirty-nine. She hated being late.

Families milled around the entrance. Parents hailed grandparents, and young children—too young to be taking part in the program—chased after each other.

The festive atmosphere lifted Pam's spirits. Her headache had abated to a dull pain behind her temples, but she still didn't want to be there. If she hadn't promised Jed, she'd be at home, in her sweatpants, snuggling with Leopold on the sofa while she surfed the internet for design ideas.

Pam skirted the crowd at the entrance and spotted Jed up ahead. She stuck to the wall of the building as she made her way to him. A familiar voice emanated from an open door on her left. She stopped in her tracks.

"I was happy to give you a ride when you had a flat tire, Susan, but that's all it was." Steve's voice carried to where Pam hovered just beyond the open door.

She heard Susan Wilbanks's sultry voice but couldn't make out the words. Pam leaned closer to the opening. She looked up at the placard over the door. It read 'Program Coordinator.'

"I'm sorry if you misunderstood," Steve replied, sounding anything but sorry. "I'm in a relationship—or at least I thought I was. At any rate, I'm not interested in going out with you, even if you were officially divorced, which you aren't."

Susan's tone turned simpering.

Pam pushed her hair off her forehead. She'd seen Steve giving Susan a ride home. They hadn't been on a date.

She felt weak with stupidity and regret.

When she glanced again at the placard above the door, she saw that Steve was in charge of this Saturday evening soccer program for kids.

How did she not know that?

Steve continued talking. "Look, Sean is a great kid, and he's shaping up to be an excellent player. I'm glad he's in the program, but please don't make this awkward."

Pam heard a chair scraping against the floor as Steve pushed it back from his desk and stood.

"I've got to go open the tournament," Steve said.

Susan stalked out of the office and stormed past Pam without noticing her.

Steve followed on her heels.

Pam stepped forward quickly and touched his arm.

"Hi," she said, her mind still reeling from what she'd just learned.

"You ready?" he asked in clipped tones.

"You bet." She fell in next to him. "I went home and watched the tape of our show about a million times," she said. "You're really good. It went so much better with the two of us."

He nodded but didn't speak. He led them to where Jed stood next to a microphone. Eight teams, together with their families, were gathered in front of them.

Steve tapped the microphone, sending an electronic screech that stopped all conversations. "Welcome to the fifth annual Linden Falls soccer tournament. Thank you to all the players—and their families—who have taken part this season."

He turned to Jed and put his hand on Jed's shoulder. "I'd also like to thank Duncan's Hardware for supporting our program and sponsoring this tournament."

A ripple of applause traveled through the crowd.

Jed took Steve's place at the microphone. "Duncan's is proud to support this tournament as we look forward to showcasing our community in even more expansive ways. As you've undoubtedly heard, we're sponsoring the new television show *Wishes of Home*. If you watched the first episode this morning, you know it's going to be a big hit. If not, set your DVRs for ten on Saturday mornings. You won't want to miss it. With me today are the co-hosts and stars of the show—Linden Falls' own Pam Olson and Steve Turner!"

He stepped back and swept them forward. The crowd responded with cheers, whistles, and enthusiastic clapping.

Steve slipped his arm around Pam's shoulders. She leaned into him as they held up their hands and waved.

As the applause died down, he dropped his arm.

Steve spoke into the microphone. "All right! Let's get this tournament started. I've posted the field assignments for the first round on the boards on either side of us. Find your team and take the field. Good luck, everyone, and remember to have fun!"

The crowd dispersed like water escaping a dam. Children in matching T-shirts swept off together, followed by parents pushing strollers and grandparents corralling preschoolers.

Pam looked at the scene in front of them. "You run this program?"

"Yeah. Of course. Didn't you know that?"

She shook her head slowly.

"I've done it for years. I thought everybody knew." He looked at her. "I started this program to give back to disadvantaged youth. It's grown to the point where kids from all backgrounds want to participate."

"I can see that. You should be very proud."

"Didn't you wonder why we never went out on Saturday nights?"

Pam felt her cheeks grow warm. "It bothered me."

"What did you think I was doing?"

She shrugged. "I figured you must be going out with someone else." She hesitated, then continued. "In fact, I was driving by the square a couple of Saturdays ago and saw you with Susan Wilbanks—in your car."

Steve recoiled as if someone had slapped him. "And you thought I was going out with *Susan*?"

Pam nodded.

"Well, that's grand. Why in the hell didn't you ask me what I was doing on Saturday nights? You should have done it weeks ago." His voice was steely.

"I… I don't know. I should have. I guess…"

"You were afraid I'd lie to you, weren't you? You didn't trust me to give you an honest answer."

"I'm so sorry, Steve." She reached for his arm, but he pulled it back.

He glared at her.

"I should have asked."

"Yes. You should have."

"Can we talk about this? Do you want to come over after the tournament?"

He shook his head slowly. "Now you want to talk? After making me feel so confused all week? I don't know, Pam. I need time to think."

"Please, Steve. Give me a chance to explain."

"Like you gave me a chance?" He looked at the fields in front of them, his expression sad. "I've got to go. I have a tournament to run."

PAM RETREATED to the wall next to his now-empty office and stared at Steve's back as he walked away. He was upset, and she understood why. She shouldn't have made assumptions. Why hadn't she talked to him? She knew that communication was the key element of a relationship and yet, she'd failed at it.

She'd been stupid—and now she was paying the price.

She slumped against the wall and closed her eyes.

There had to be something she could do or say to apologize and get them back on track.

She inhaled deeply and opened her eyes to find a young girl staring at her.

"You're the TV lady, aren't you? The one on that new show?"

Pam stood up straight. She was looking at Laura Thompson.

"Yes. I am. And you're the girl who was at the farmer's market a couple of weeks ago—collecting money to build a no-kill animal shelter in Linden Falls."

Laura smiled shyly. "That's me. You came by my table, didn't you?"

"I did. I wanted to give you money." Pam withdrew her wallet from her purse. "But when I went back to find you, you were gone. I looked for you the next week, too."

"My brother got bored and made us leave early. He had soccer practice on the Saturdays after that, so I haven't been back."

"Is your brother in the tournament?"

Laura nodded. "My mom gave me money for the vending machine." She rattled coins in her hand.

"Are you still collecting money for the shelter?" Pam pulled a twenty-dollar bill from her wallet.

"No. I only got eleven dollars and my mom said we'd never get enough, so we sent what we'd collected to the shelter where we got my dog. Mom asked them what it would take to turn the shelter into the kind where no animals get killed. The lady on the phone said they would love to do that, but it can't happen." Laura's smile dimmed. "We just gave them the money for food."

"Your heart is in the right place, that's for sure," Pam

said, putting her money back into her purse.

"Mom says that even if I can't raise enough money to build the shelter, I should keep wishing for my dream."

"Did you tie a wish to the Wishing Tree?"

"Yes! How do you know that?"

"I saw it."

Laura dragged her toe along the pavement in front of her. "Do you believe in the Wishing Tree?"

Pam responded without hesitation. "I sure do." She glanced in the direction that Steve had gone.

"You know what else I'm wishing for?"

"What's that?"

"That someone came along right after us and took home the other dog I wanted. He was a ginormous black lab with one white eyebrow. Mom said he was too big for us. We live in an apartment."

Pam's heart turned over.

"Mom also says to keep wishing. She says that just because we don't see a way to make something happen doesn't mean someone else won't come along who does."

"Your mom sounds very wise."

Laura nodded. "I'd better get my snack and go back to my parents." She headed for the vending machine.

Pam watched Laura go. The determination in those little shoulders struck a responsive chord in her. Hadn't Irene always remarked on Pam's tenacity?

An idea began forming in her brain. "Laura," she called. "What's the name of that shelter where you got your dog?"

Laura spun around and gave Pam the information.

"Thank you." She inhaled slowly. She was going to be that someone to help make Laura's dream come true.

CHAPTER 21

"*T*hat's a wrap for the week," Marty called. "Good work, everyone. We're in the groove, now."

Steve sprinted down Irene's front steps.

Pam followed and caught up to him at the sidewalk. Somehow, in front of the camera, they were able to find the easy camaraderie they'd always had, their banter natural and automatic. But as soon as the scenes were over, it turned icy again.

"You're still upset with me, aren't you?"

Steve stopped and looked down at her, raking his fingers through his hair. "To be honest, I've been so busy with my clients at the gym and this gig," he gestured toward the house with his head, "that I haven't had time to figure out how I feel."

Pam remained silent, waiting for him to continue.

"You said—when you thought I was seeing someone else—that you wanted to wait until filming of your mom's remodel was done to talk about this. I think that's a good plan. We have to work together on this show. It's awkward enough as it is. Let's not risk making it worse."

"Talking could also make things better, you know." Pam stepped closer. "I'm sorry, Steve. I should have trusted you."

Steve moved away and held up both hands, palms facing out. "Not here and not now. Like I said, we need to wait." He turned his back on her and continued to his car.

Pam watched until the shadows enveloped him before she trudged to her car in the opposite direction. She made her way home to another fitful night of sleep.

PAM'S PHONE buzzed with an incoming call. She slung the grocery bags in her arms onto her kitchen counter and retrieved her phone from her purse just before it would have clicked over to voice mail.

"Pam. It's Carol—Steve's sister."

"Hi! How are you?"

"Great. Busy, as always. I'm sorry I haven't called earlier—to congratulate you on the success of the show. You and Steve have become quite the local celebrities."

"I don't know about that," Pam laughed. "But thank you. It's fun."

"Your mother's bathroom looks fabulous. I'd like to pick your brain on new counters and backsplash for my kitchen."

"I'd love to—any time." Pam held the phone to her ear with her shoulder while she began unpacking her perishables.

"That's not why I'm calling. Steve's birthday is a week

from Sunday. I'm throwing a surprise party for him. Nothing fancy—just family and a few friends. You have to be there, of course."

Pam set the quart of milk she'd removed from a bag back on the counter. "I'm not sure that's a good idea."

"What—a surprise party? He'll love it."

"Not that. I meant that he probably won't want to see me there."

"What are you talking about? Have the two of you broken up?"

Pam pulled out a stool and plopped onto it. "To tell you the truth, I'm not sure."

"Oh no, please don't tell me that. You two are perfect for each other," Carol said. "If you don't mind me asking, what happened?"

Pam filled her in, ending with the events at the soccer tournament and her encounter with Steve at the conclusion of the past week's filming.

"Geez," Carol said. "It sounds like a giant misunderstanding."

"I should have asked him before I jumped to conclusions."

"Maybe—but, to be honest, I would have thought the same thing you did. You've been hurt by your cheating ex-husband and didn't want to set yourself up to be hurt again. I would probably have reacted the same way."

"Thank you, Carol. That means a lot to me, but I really need Steve to understand. And he doesn't want to talk about it right now."

The line remained silent for a beat.

"Has he said anything to you about... us?"

"Nope. Not a word. Which is just great. He'd have no reason to be mad at me if I invited you to his party."

"Won't he be upset with me if I turn up?"

"Hmmmm… maybe." She sighed. "I'm going to call that knuckle-headed brother of mine. Maybe I can talk some sense into him." Her voice wavered with emotion. "I'm not going to stand by and watch the two of you let your relationship go south over a silly misunderstanding."

"I hope it works."

"Me, too. If you come to his party, it'll give you a chance to be together."

"We see each other at the gym every weekday and we're together two nights a week for filming. I don't think that'll make any difference." Pam toyed with the torn edge on one of her grocery sacks. "Why don't I drop off a gift for him before the party starts? A sort of peace offering."

"That's not a bad idea. He'll contact you to say thank you."

"Any idea what he might want?"

"You know—I've got just the thing. You're not going to believe it, but I think Steve would love a dog. A big dog. It's been a family joke for years that he always asked for a dog for his birthday or Christmas, but he never got one. Our nana lived with us growing up and she was allergic to dogs."

Pam chuckled. "That's a wonderful idea. I've heard him talk about always wanting a dog but never getting one. I'm going for broke with this gift, so what's the worst that can happen? He gets mad at me for foisting a dog on him? He's mad at me right now, anyway."

"If he really doesn't like the dog, we'll take it," Carol

said. "Our family is dog-crazy and the kids have been begging to get another one."

"It's settled, then. And I know just where I'm going to get the dog."

Pam knew that with Steve's soft heart, a rescue dog would mean the most to him.

"Great," Carol said. "Steve thinks he's just coming over for lunch on his birthday. He'll be here by noon but I'm telling guests to arrive by eleven-thirty."

"Sounds perfect. I'll bring the dog to your house by eleven."

"Don't you want to stay—to see his reaction to your gift?"

Pam paused, considering this. "No. That seems like I'd be putting pressure on him. Like those very public proposals on the jumbotron at a ball game. I often wonder if the person says yes because they're too self-conscious to create a scene by saying no. I'll write a note on a birthday card. If he wants to call me, he can."

"It's a plan." Carol's voice became firm. "If I have anything to do with it, you'll be back together in no time."

CHAPTER 22

*P*am entered Friends for Life animal shelter an hour before closing time on Sunday afternoon. The earthy aroma of dog and cat enveloped her as soon as she opened the door. Yipping and barking emanated from the back of the building.

"I know you close in an hour," she said to the older woman at the reception desk who wore a tag that said she was the volunteer of the month. "Is there still enough time for me to look for a dog?"

"Sure," the woman said. "You go right on back, honey. We'll close our front door at four, but we'll be here as long as it takes to process paperwork for anyone who wants to give one of our dogs or cats a good home. Take your time. Nothing makes us happier than when we can place one of our animals."

"Thank you," Pam said. She'd intended to get there earlier in the afternoon but had lost track of time as she'd finished painting Irene's bathroom.

The woman pointed to two doors behind her labeled

DOGS and CATS, respectively. "If you find an animal you like, let one of the staff know and they'll put the two of you in a get-acquainted room."

Pam nodded and walked into the dog area. She sauntered up and down the rows of cages. A handful of other people were shopping for a dog on this late Sunday afternoon, too.

Tails wagged and noses pressed themselves through the metal grids of their cages. Most of the dogs were small mixed breeds. Dark eyes and noses set in shaggy white fur melted her heart. She didn't know how Leopold would react to a canine companion, but Pam could see herself with any of the sweet creatures striving to gain her attention. She didn't see Steve with a small dog, however, and continued looking. No one else seemed to be interested in the larger breeds.

She passed a pen with a big dog. The placard on the cage said she was a purebred German shepherd. She stayed in the back of her cage.

Pam felt sure someone would adopt the beautiful animal based on her looks and pedigree.

The next pen held a dog that looked to be a poodle mix. His placard said he was eleven years old. She quickly turned her eyes away from the dog's, praying that a senior citizen looking for a pet in a similar stage of its life would adopt this dog.

Pam wanted a younger companion for Steve.

The third pen held a black lab mix. He was sleeping on his side. His head reached the back of the pen while his hind paws touched the front. He was enormous. She read the placard. He was eighteen months old. His coat was deepest black and shone like a seal's.

Pam signaled to a young man wearing coveralls embroidered with the words 'Friends for Life Staff.'

"Would you like to get to know this guy?"

"Yes. I hate to wake him up, but yes."

"Trust me, he won't mind. He's one of the best dogs we've ever had—very easy going. Come on, Chance," the man said, entering the pen and slipping a leash around the dog's neck.

The dog leapt to his feet, shook himself, and turned to face Pam.

She gasped. The dog had a strip of white fur over one eye—making it look like he had a white eyebrow. Was it possible that this was the big dog that Laura had wanted to adopt? Surely not—that dog had been scheduled for euthanasia the day after Laura's visit.

Pam followed the man to a small room at the end of the hallway. He ushered Chance inside and she followed.

When she dropped to one knee and held out her hands to the dog, it came to her without hesitation and licked her face with a slobbery pass of his tongue.

Pam pulled away, laughing and wiping away the spit with her hand.

She stood and took the leash.

Chance fell in beside her as she walked around the small room, matching her step for step.

"He's leash trained, isn't he?"

"And housebroken. He knows sit, stay, and down, too."

"What happened to him? Do you know why he's here?"

"He was picked up as a stray. He's a great dog and I'd take him home myself if I didn't already have seven." He smiled ruefully. "That's one problem with working here."

"I'm surprised someone didn't adopt him this weekend."

"We are, too. In fact, we've had him here for almost two months. He was supposed to be put down over a month ago. He's such a wonderful dog that no one had the heart to do it."

Shivers ran down Pam's spine. This was the same dog Laura had wanted.

"We think no one's taken him because he's so big. Most people don't have room for a guy this size."

Chance looked up at the man and wagged his tail as if he agreed with him.

"That's why we named him Chance—we want someone to take a chance on him."

She leaned over and looked into the dog's soulful brown eyes. He needed a second chance—just like she did with Steve. "I'll take him," she said. "Chance is coming home with me."

A smile exploded on the man's face. "That's beyond wonderful." He choked on the words. "This might have been his last weekend."

Chance reacted to the man's emotion, wagging his tail so hard that a stiff breeze whirled around their knees.

"We're full and we have to do something to bring our numbers down. We're only licensed for a certain number of animals. Shelters from other areas sometimes pick up dogs before we have to put them down, but they rarely take the big guys."

They made their way to a waiting room. "You can take a seat." He pointed to a row of molded plastic chairs that lined one wall.

An older couple, cradling what looked like a dachshund terrier mix, were the only other people around.

"Someone will come get you to complete the paperwork," the man said.

He dropped to one knee and put his arms around the dog's neck, pressing his face into Chance's fur. "I told you we'd find you a forever home," he said, his voice thick.

He stood and looked at Pam. "You've got yourself a great dog."

"Thank you," Pam said, swallowing back the tears that this display of emotion had triggered. "He'll be well taken care of."

The man rubbed the back of his hand across his eyes.

"This must be a very hard job," Pam said quietly.

"Sometimes it is. It's very gratifying to see animals go out for adoption." He glanced at the couple, cooing over the small dog, who was wagging its tail and showering them with kisses. "Pets bring people immeasurable happiness. The reality that they can't all find homes—that we sometimes have to put an animal to sleep—is... well... it sucks. We shouldn't have let Chance here stay as long as we did."

"I'm so grateful that you took a..." She smiled. "A chance on Chance."

"Me too. You have no idea how excited everyone will be tomorrow when they come in to find that he's been adopted."

"There are no-kill shelters," Pam said. "Why don't you make Friends for Life into a no-kill one?"

"Space," he answered quickly. "We simply don't have enough room for all the animals if we did that."

"Sounds like you've looked into it?"

"Yes—we're continually trying to find a way. We have a good idea how many animals we'd have to accommodate. We have the staffing and could raise the money to feed them. We just can't house them."

"How much more space do you think you'd need?"

"Another three thousand square feet." He shook his head sadly. "We don't have the funding to acquire and outfit it."

Pam stared past him, thinking.

"We keep wishing for a miracle."

Pam snapped out of her reverie. There it was, again: that idea of wishing for a no-kill shelter.

Two staff members entered the room from the other end. One beckoned to the couple with the dachshund and the other spoke to Pam. "Let's get the two of you taken care of," the woman said.

Pam reached out and touched the young man's arm. "Thank you, again, for saving Chance for me."

CHAPTER 23

"When you're finished with your homework, you can watch TV," Carol said to her children, who were sprawled on their beds or sitting at desks in their rooms. "I need to call Uncle Steve."

Carol took her cell phone and retreated to her bedroom. She'd replayed her conversation with Pam in her mind at least a dozen times.

Pam still cared for her brother and Carol was convinced Pam was Steve's soul mate. Her brother wasn't going to miss out on a happy future with this woman if Carol had anything to do with it. Steve didn't usually confide his problems, but she had to try to find out what was bothering him.

Steve's phone rang as he left the gym at eight o'clock on Monday night. The ring tone told him that his sister was calling.

"Hey, Sis. What's up?"

"Just confirming that you're coming for lunch on Sunday at noon. Will you bring Pam? It's your birthday and Mom and Dad will be here, too. They're dying to meet her."

"I'll be there. As far as it being my birthday, we can forget all about that."

"You know you don't mean that. I've never seen anyone who loves a box-mix birthday cake more than you."

Steve chuckled. "Okay—you've got me there. I'm a big fan. I just don't want you to go to a lot of trouble."

"Me—fuss over you? Never." She paused, then continued. "Seriously, are you bringing Pam?"

The line remained silent, then Steve replied. "I don't think so. Pam and I are… taking a break right now."

"What? You look like you're getting along great together on the show."

"We're fine—on-screen."

"Then why are you taking a break?" She held her breath, waiting for him to tell her he didn't want to talk about it.

"Trust is a big issue with me. You know that."

"Yes. So—what has Pam done to destroy that trust? Is she seeing someone else?" Carol asked, knowing that Pam was doing no such thing.

"It's nothing like that. She jumped to a conclusion about me that wasn't warranted—and she didn't trust me enough to ask me about it."

"Now you're being cryptic." Carol plumped the pillows against the headboard, settling herself against them and bringing her knees up to her chest. "I need details."

Steve filled her in on Pam's misunderstanding of his Saturday night commitments and her incorrectly thinking he was involved with Susan Wilbanks. "She wouldn't talk about it. I didn't have a chance to explain."

"I'll grant you that she should have listened to your side of the story, but I can understand why she came to those conclusions."

"Oh, come on. Everyone knows I run the soccer program on Saturday nights."

"Not everyone. Pam didn't. She's still fairly new in town, remember? And she's probably not around anyone involved with your program. Be reasonable, Steve. You could've mentioned it to her, you know." Carol snuggled deeper into the pillows.

"I didn't want to look like I was bragging or trying to get attention for my volunteer work," he said. "I just assumed she knew."

"Hmm," Carol said. "I get that, but seeing you with Susan in your car? If the situation were reversed, you would have thought the same thing she did. I know I would have." She paused, listening to him breathing deeply.

"You may be right. But why wouldn't she have talked to me about it? She cut me out. I asked what was wrong. She said that she was busy with the show and wanted to get through with that first."

"I agree with you one hundred percent—she should have talked to you. Communication is important. But let's unpack this. She saw you with Susan—who the whole town knows is always looking for something or someone to entertain her—when Pam was unbelievably stressed about the show. She thought she was going to cause the show to fail—and evidently, she was right because they brought you in."

"That's true."

"She was essentially working two jobs and suddenly dealing with what she thought was a cheating boyfriend. Talk about stress! I can understand her feeling completely overwhelmed."

"I hadn't thought about it like that."

"Pam didn't refuse to talk to you, did she? She asked you to wait until the show was done filming in a few weeks."

"I assumed that meant she'd never talk about it."

"Ah ha! You're making assumptions, too."

"Bottom line, Carol, is that I want a relationship with someone who will talk to me when there are problems. Not ghost me."

"Of course you do."

"You and Tom are terrific communicators."

"Thank you. We are—mostly. But we didn't start out that way. We've had to learn that skill over the course of our marriage and we still work on it all the time."

"What are you saying?"

"You know I don't meddle in your business."

"That's true."

"And I want the very best for you."

"I know that."

Carol sat up straight on the bed and delivered her next words with conviction. "I think you and Pam are made for each other. You've both been deeply hurt in the past, which may make both of you hesitant moving forward with someone else. I look at what you've just told me as a miscommunication—with fault on both sides. I wouldn't give up on her so quickly."

"I appreciate where you're coming from," Steve said, "but I'm not so sure. I need to think about it."

"Will you invite her to lunch on Sunday?"

"With the folks? No. She and I will need to talk first."

"Okay. I'll see you Sunday."

"I'll be there. And I'll consider what you said. Thanks for being such a concerned sister."

"Always." Carol tapped off the call and got to her feet. She'd planted seeds she prayed would take root.

CHAPTER 24

*P*am re-read for the umpteenth time the note she'd penned to Steve, then folded it in half and inserted it into the birthday card. She licked the flap to seal it.

Chance lay on the rug at her feet, with Leopold nestled on the back of the sofa where Pam sat. Leopold had not welcomed Chance with open arms. However, he was no longer constantly hissing and spitting at the dog who appeared unfazed by the cat. Given more time, she thought they might even become friends.

Pam got to her feet and gathered up the prior drafts of the note that she had crumpled and tossed to the floor before she'd been satisfied with the final version. "Come on, Chance. Time to go. This is your big moment."

Chance sprang to his feet, tail wagging.

Pam discarded the papers in the kitchen trash, turned to the huge pup, and clipped on his leash. She stroked his silky ears. "You've been such a good boy. You're going to be a birthday gift for a very special man. I think he's wanted you his whole life."

Chance lifted his eyes to hers and wagged his tail.

"If he doesn't want you, you're coming right back here —to me. Do you understand? You're never going back to a shelter. You could also stay with the family I'm taking you to now. They offered. But I've decided I want you back if Steve doesn't keep you."

He emitted a short "woof."

Pam led him to her SUV and put him in the back seat. They pulled up in front of Carol's house shortly before eleven.

Ben threw open the front door before Pam and Chance were halfway up the driveway. Riley was on Ben's heels. "We're going to hide him in my room," Ben said, racing to meet them, barely able to contain his excitement.

Pam followed Ben and Riley into the house. She gave Chance one last pat and handed the leash to Ben.

"He's sure big," Riley said as the boys started up the stairs.

Chance charged alongside them without a backward glance at Pam.

Carol called out from the kitchen.

"I'm racing around, trying to finish this cake before the guests arrive. I hope no one's late and that they all park around the corner. Steve notices everything. I don't want him to guess that this is a surprise party." Carol piped the last bit of decorative icing on the cake and finished with a flourish. "There," she said, stepping back to admire her handiwork.

"That's beautiful," Pam said. "It's like something out of one of those baking shows."

Carol flushed with pleasure. "Thanks."

"Do you need help with anything?" Pam asked.

"Nope." Carol rinsed her sticky hands under the faucet and untied her apron. "Did the boys take the dog?"

Pam nodded. "Chance went with them as if he didn't have a care in the world. Looks like I worried needlessly that he'd have separation anxiety."

She reached into her purse and handed Carol the card. "Will you please give this to Steve when he sees Chance?"

"Why don't you stay and give it to him yourself?"

"I don't think that's wise," Pam said. "We have to be together during filming next week and that's awkward enough. I don't want to force myself on him. If he wants to see me, he knows where to find me. I cover all of that in the card."

Carol nodded. "I'm hoping—no, I'm praying—that the two of you work this out."

"Me, too," Pam said. "I'd better go. I parked my car in your driveway. I don't want your other guests to see my vehicle and think it's okay."

Carol walked with Pam and gave her a hug in the doorway.

"Have a wonderful party," Pam said. "And if Steve doesn't want Chance, let me know. I'll take him back in a heartbeat."

"Will do. I'm hoping that when he meets Chance and reads your card, he'll sneak out of this party early to find you."

Pam laughed. "If he does, will you send him with a piece of that cake?"

～

STEVE DROVE down the street behind his sister's house. He usually approached from the other direction. He was surprised to see that both sides of the street were lined with cars. Someone must be having a party, he thought as he pulled into Carol's driveway and parked next to his parent's car.

He slammed his car door. Deep-throated barking emanated from the second floor. It didn't sound like Sugar, his sister's elderly golden retriever.

Had Carol and Tom finally given in to their kids' pleas and gotten a new dog?

Steve mounted the front steps and knocked lightly on the door before pushing it open and crossing the threshold. The foyer was empty. "Hello," he called.

No one answered. More barking rang out from the floor above him. He headed for the kitchen. A beautiful cake stood on the island. "Carol?" He raised his voice.

"Out back," came her response.

Steve opened the patio door. Thirty of his closest friends and family surged toward him, all hollering, "Surprise!"

He bent slightly, putting his hands on his thighs, and laughed. He should've known and if he hadn't been so preoccupied with thoughts about Pam, he would've. It was so like his sister to pull off a surprise party.

Carol raced to him and swept him into a hug. "Happy Birthday, little bro," she said into his ear. She pulled back to look into his face. "Were you really surprised?"

"I was. I even came in that way." He pointed to the

street behind hers. "And saw all the cars. Is that where you told people to park?"

Carol nodded. "That didn't tip you off?"

"Nope. I thought someone must be having a party, but I didn't think it was you hosting one for me."

"Good. Everyone's waiting to say hello to you. Then we'll eat lunch and cut the cake."

His sister headed for the kitchen to set out food while Steve shook hands and got clapped on the back.

"I can't believe you didn't let on," he teased his mother as he hugged her.

"I can keep my mouth shut when I need to," she said. "And this isn't the only surprise of the day."

Steve raised an eyebrow.

"You'll have to wait a bit for the rest."

He cocked his head to one side and narrowed his eyes at his mother. "How about a hint?"

She wagged her finger at him and shook her head.

Carol emerged from the kitchen and led him to the front of the buffet line set up in the kitchen. "Start us off, birthday boy," she said.

"BBQ—with all the trimmings," Steve said. "My favorite. Thank you—both," he said as Tom came to stand behind his wife.

"I'm hoping we can do this for your birthday every year," Tom said. "It's the only time this one," he gestured to his wife, "will let me go off my diet and have BBQ."

"Glad to be of service," Steve said, filling his plate.

"We've set up tables on the patio," Carol announced as the kitchen filled with hungry guests. "Beverages are out there, too."

Steve cleaned his plate and went back for seconds. He

made his way from table to table, chatting with his friends.

He noticed his niece and nephew imploring his mother to do something with increasing regularity.

Carol kept shaking her head 'no.' He was finally close enough to hear her say "after the cake."

The three kids raced off, giggling conspiratorially.

Carol stood and went into the house, returning with her beautiful cake. She placed it on a table off to one side which had been set with cake plates, forks, napkins, and a cake knife.

Then she picked up the knife and struck a glass with it to get everyone's attention. "It's time to cut the cake," she said. "Fire department regulations prohibit us from using the correct number of candles."

The kids snickered at this time-worn joke.

"We'll have to make do with one candle."

Tom reached in and lit the lone taper in the center of the cake. Everyone sang "Happy Birthday to You."

Steve stood and squeezed his eyes shut, making a show of conjuring up his wish.

"Blow it out, Uncle Steve," Emma whispered from behind him.

Steve leaned over and blew out the candle. The group clapped and whistled.

Carol cut the first slice, put it and a fork on a plate, and handed it to Steve.

The kids fell in line next to her, ready to ferry cake to their guests.

Carol served a second slice and set it to one side.

"Who's that for?" Ben asked.

Carol just smiled at him and prepared another plate.

The party continued until midafternoon. Steve said goodbye to the last of his friends and then walked around the corner to bring his parents' car to them.

After they left, he headed for the kitchen.

Carol and Tom stood arm in arm as the kids bounced with excitement.

"Okay," Steve said. "You're keeping something from me, aren't you?"

The kids turned to their parents, looking for all the world like thoroughbreds in the starting gate.

Tom nodded, and all three of them raced up the stairs.

Steve heard more of the deep baritone barking, followed by the thundering sound of three children and one gigantic dog coming down the stairs.

Chance burst into the kitchen and headed straight for Steve.

Steve took a step back as the dog raised on his back feet and lunged for him. He caught Chance's front paws and placed them on the ground. "Whoa, boy," he said, kneeling to pet the squirming animal.

Chance showered him with slobbery kisses.

Steve turned his head this way and that, laughing.

"I thought I heard unfamiliar barking in the house when I got here," he said. "When did you get a new dog?"

"We didn't," Carol said, pointing to the red bow the kids had attached to his collar right before they brought him downstairs. "He's for you."

Steve stared at her, his expression one of a small boy getting a dog for his birthday.

"Do you like him?"

Steve was already on the ground, wrestling with Chance.

Carol's eyes filled with tears. She watched as Ben and Riley joined the fracas.

Steve finally stood, commanding the dog to sit. He reached for the tag on his collar and examined the name. "Chance," he said, looking at the dog carefully. "I think that's a good name for you." He turned to his family. "Thank you so much for this guy."

"He's not from us," Emma blurted out. "He's from your girlfriend."

Steve looked at Carol.

She nodded. "Pam got him for you. He's a rescue, by the way. His papers are in this card that she dropped off for you."

Steve took the envelope she held out to him.

"Open it," the kids said in unison.

"I think Steve needs to read it on his own," Carol said.

He turned the envelope over in his hands. "Your mother is right," he said, his voice hoarse. "I'll help you clean up, then Chance and I will get out of your hair. I'll read it when I get home."

"You are not helping clean up your own party," Tom said. "The kids and I will do it." He addressed his wife. "You've been working since before dawn. Go soak in the tub with your book."

Carol stood on tiptoes to kiss his cheek. "I'm not going to say 'no' to that." She took her brother's arm and walked him and Chance to his SUV.

"I think this dog is aptly named," she said. "He needed a second chance at finding a forever home, and you and Pam should give your relationship a second chance."

"I'll read this," he said, holding up the card.

Carol took his face in her hands. "Let yourself be happy, Steve. You deserve it."

"Thanks for a wonderful party, Sis. The food was great and I appreciate all the time and effort you and Tom put into it."

"You're welcome." She spun him around toward his car. "Now go. I think there's a woman who's anxiously waiting to hear from you."

CHAPTER 25

*S*teve turned toward home, with Chance on the passenger seat next to him. He'd made a half-hearted attempt to put the big dog in the back seat, but Chance had stepped over the console between the front seats and settled in next to Steve—like that's where he belonged.

The envelope with his name written in Pam's familiar scrawl lay on the dashboard in front of him.

He shifted his gaze from the envelope to Chance and back again, then pulled off the street into the deserted parking lot of an office building.

Steve put his car in park and snatched the envelope.

Chance pushed himself up into a sitting position, sensing this change in energy from his human. He pointed his nose at Steve, his mouth open as he panted.

Steve scratched behind Chance's ears, then unsealed the envelope. The card had a close-up photo of a black lab with a yearning expression. A white eyebrow had been drawn in and the photo bore an uncanny likeness to

Chance. The message printed inside the card read: *There's no one I'd rather be with than you! Happy Birthday!* She'd signed it simply: *Love, Pam.*

The envelope contained two folded pieces of paper. The first was Chance's adoption paperwork from Friends for Life.

Steve scanned it briefly, noting it contained his immunization records, approximate age, and weight. He'd thought the dog was a hundred pounder and smiled when he saw he'd been correct—the paper recorded a weight of one hundred eight pounds.

He tossed the card and adoption paperwork on the dashboard and turned to Pam's handwritten note.

He unfolded it carefully, took a deep breath, and began to read.

Dearest Steve,

I am so very sorry that I jumped to incorrect and unwarranted conclusions. I'm doubly sorry that I didn't give you a chance to explain. The reasons I did all of this really don't matter. I can't undo anything now.

I was (am) in love with you and am hoping we can find our way back to each other. I pray you forgive me and give us a second chance.

I'd been toying with ways to present this to you when Carol called about your surprise party. She told me you'd always wanted a dog, and we agreed I would get you one. When I went to the shelter and found the big guy who I assume is with you now, I knew he was the dog for you. When I learned his name was Chance, that sealed the deal.

The shelter workers named him Chance. They'd taken a chance on him by letting him stay a month beyond the date when he should have been put to sleep. He's the dog that the

165

little girl from the Wishing Tree was talking about in her wish. Isn't that wild?

Suddenly, we're surrounded by second chances. Will you give us one?

Love,

Pam

P.S. If you don't want to keep Chance, no problem. I realize it's a big risk, giving someone a dog. I'll take him back in a heartbeat. I've got a big bag of dog food for him at my house. You're welcome to stop by for it or I can bring it to you. If you don't want to see me, I can leave it by your front door. xx

Steve re-read the note, then turned to Chance. "What do you think, big guy?"

Chance swept his tail along the seat.

"Do you like Pam?"

Chance woofed.

"Is she the one for me?"

Chance barked louder.

"Carol thinks so. I do, too." Steve put his SUV in gear. "We've got a quick stop to make and then we're headed to Pam's."

Chance turned his face to the passenger side window. Steve rolled it down and Chance stuck his head out, enjoying the breeze on his face in the way only dogs can do.

They arrived back at Carol's in under ten minutes. "Wait here, Chance," Steve said. "I'm only going in for a minute."

Chance woofed in agreement.

Carol was wiping down the counter when Steve entered the kitchen. She looked at him in surprise. "Forget something?"

"I was wondering if you had any of that cake left? I'd like to take a piece to Pam."

Carol tossed her dishrag on the counter and crossed to her brother, throwing her arms around him. "Does this mean that you read her card and are going to see her?"

Steve nodded. "If you ever mention to anyone else that I said this, I'll deny it, but you were right. It would be a colossal mistake not to give our relationship a second chance."

Carol stared at him with shining eyes. "I'm beyond thrilled. And," she walked to the pantry and pulled down from a tall shelf a piece of cake on a paper plate, wrapped in cellophane, "I saved this for Pam. I promised her a slice when she dropped the dog off. I was hiding it from Tom and the kids."

Steve laughed. "Thank you."

"The rest of the cake got eaten, but I have leftovers of everything else in the fridge." She grabbed a handled shopping bag and removed a handful of carryout containers from the refrigerator, stacking them in the bag. "Are you headed to Pam's now?"

"I am."

"Then you'll have plenty for the two of you." She kissed his cheek. "I'm so glad about all of this. I think you're on the way to the happy life you deserve."

"And I thought you were going to take one of your long bubble baths. You've worked hard today—it's time for you to quit cleaning up the kitchen and go relax."

"Point well taken. I'm on my way. Let me know how everything goes."

PAM WAS TRIMMING the rose bushes along her rear fence when she heard the familiar baritone barking. She dropped her secateurs and wiped her grimy hands along the legs of her jeans, wishing she'd heeded her mother's advice to always wear gloves when she worked in the garden.

Her T-shirt was stuck to her back with sweat and her hair hung in limp hanks around her shoulders. She'd attacked her overgrown garden with gusto to take her mind off what Steve might—or might not—be thinking about her note and her gift of Chance. Whether he was here to make up or break up for good, she didn't want him to see her looking so rough.

She ran to her back porch and raced into the house as the doorbell rang. She rinsed her hands in the kitchen sink and dabbed her damp face with a paper towel, then ran it inside her shirt to swipe at each armpit.

The doorbell sounded again.

Pam deposited the paper towel in the trash, twisted her hair into a messy bun that she secured with a hair tie she dug out of her pocket, and went to the door.

Steve stood on the porch, a huge black dog on one side of himself and a grocery bag on the other.

She looked into his eyes, and his expression gave her the answer she longed for.

He crossed the distance between them in one stride and took her into his arms.

They held each other with increasing fervor until Steve rocked back, took her face in both of his hands, and kissed her long and slow.

A shiny wet nose finally inserted itself between them, followed by a generous tongue lashing.

Pam and Steve stepped apart.

"Down, boy," Steve said, pushing Chance's front paws back to the floor. "If you want to hang with me, you can't interrupt moments like this."

Pam laughed and bent to pet the dog, who was wagging his tail and squirming at their feet. "Do you like him?"

"Are you kidding? He's the best birthday present—no, make that any kind of present—I've ever received."

"I'm thrilled. He's great—I love him already—but I wasn't sure if you wanted to take on the responsibility that goes along with a dog."

"I think I'm ready to settle down," Steve said, a teasing tone in his voice. "Seriously, I'm glad you took the chance —no pun intended—on him."

"Do you want to come in?" Pam stepped into the house and Chance raced inside.

Steve picked up the grocery sack. "I'm delivering to you a piece of the best birthday cake in town from Carol."

"Oh, yeah! It looked great. I'll be sure to thank her."

"She also sent this entire bag of leftover BBQ. Are you hungry?"

"I am, but didn't you just have that for lunch?"

"I did. It was great."

"You won't want it again for dinner, will you?"

"What are you talking about? I could eat BBQ three meals a day." He brought the grocery sack into the kitchen.

They worked together as they warmed up the leftovers.

Pam fed Chance while Steve told her about the party.

When they'd filled their plates, they took them to the wrought-iron table on the patio.

"I know I wrote this in my note, but I want to say it to your face, Steve. I'm sorry. I shouldn't have doubted you."

Steve took her hand and brought it to his lips. "I know Lance cheated on you and hurt you horribly. I would never do that to you. It's not who I am."

"I know that," Pam said. "I should have…"

Steve leaned in and kissed her. "You know what I think?"

She shrugged, their faces inches apart.

"You were overly tired and stressed by the show."

"I was," she whispered. "All of that clouded my judgment."

"And then circumstantial evidence presented itself and you drew the wrong conclusion."

"That's exactly it. And I wouldn't even talk to you about it. Like I said, I'm so sorry. This was all my fault."

"Not really. I stupidly assumed you knew I ran the Saturday-night soccer program. That was pretty arrogant of me."

"I wondered why we never went out on Saturday nights."

"I'm always so busy running the program that I wouldn't have any time to spend with you. That's why I never invited you. I figured you'd be bored. You work so hard all week—I thought you'd be happier at home with your HGTV and Leopold."

Pam laughed. "That's true."

"And then when you found out what was keeping me busy on Saturday night—and that I wasn't having a fling with Susan," he shuddered, "you wanted to talk, but I wouldn't let you. I reacted the same way you did. I can't be mad at you for doing what I did."

"We're only human. We're going to make mistakes."

They rested their foreheads together.

"We need to promise each other that we'll talk about things—no matter what." He breathed the words.

"I promise," she said.

They kissed again with growing intensity.

A high-pitched yowl followed by a yelp emanated from the house.

Pam jumped to her feet. "Leopold," Pam hollered. "Be nice."

They hurried inside to find Chance rubbing a paw across his nose as Leopold glared down at him from the top of the refrigerator.

"What happened, boy?" Steve said, dropping to one knee to examine Chance's nose.

"Is he okay?"

"There's no visible damage. I think his feelings might be hurt." He addressed Chance. "You've got to be careful around cats. They may not be as interested in you as you are in them."

"I'm surprised," Pam said. "They'd established a peaceful co-existence this week."

"I'm just glad we're back together," Steve said, sweeping Pam into his arms. "These two may need more time."

They kissed again.

"I'd better get going. We both have clients at five-thirty tomorrow morning."

"It's a good thing we have the same schedule," she said. "Let me load you up with Chance's food and other stuff."

"Other stuff?"

"Dog bed, toys, chew sticks, toothbrush, Kongs." Pam led him to a pile of items in her spare bedroom. "And a sweater."

"Sweater?" Steve sputtered with laughter. "I'm not sure this guy will ever need a sweater, but it's spring right now."

"I know," Pam said. "It was on sale and so cute." She handed him a red sweater decorated with a jolly Santa seated in a sleigh filled with presents and pulled across a glittery night sky by reindeer.

Pam pushed a button and Rudolph's nose glowed.

"An ugly Christmas sweater?"

Chance had followed them into the room.

Steve took the sweater from Pam and stuck it under his arm. "Don't worry," he said to Chance in an exaggerated stage whisper as Pam walked them to his SUV. "This thing will get lost before next Christmas. You can count on me."

Chance hopped into his now-familiar spot on the passenger seat. Pam and Steve shared a lingering kiss in her driveway before he tore himself away and headed for home.

CHAPTER 26

Steve and Pam walked up the street to Irene's house on Thursday afternoon for the last day of filming that week. They held hands, swinging them loosely between them.

"I wonder if anyone's noticed the difference between us?"

"No way," Steve said. "We were great together in front of the camera the past few weeks and kept it very professional between takes. No one will detect a difference."

"Hmmm…" she said, dropping his hand. "I'm not so sure." She shrugged. "Maybe you're right."

"Did your mother pick up on anything?"

Pam rolled her eyes. "She didn't have to. I called her the minute you left my house on Sunday."

"Silly me," Steve said. "I forgot how close the two of you are."

They turned off the sidewalk and headed up the walkway to Irene's house. Pam leaned in and whispered in Steve's ear. "Let's keep going as we have been and see if anyone mentions anything. If they do, you bring me coffee at the gym tomorrow. If they don't, I'll bring it to you."

"Extra-large, with skim and two sugars," he replied.

"I know how you like your coffee," Pam said, cuffing him on the shoulder. "Just don't be too sure of yourself."

"And don't you start looking at me all doe-eyed," he replied. "We have to maintain the same demeanor we have in the past."

Pam wagged her finger at him as she peeled off to join her hair and makeup stylists.

Filming went well, and Marty announced they were done for the week before nine o'clock. "This is the earliest we've finished to date. Good work, everyone." He hailed Pam and Steve and asked them to join him in the kitchen with Irene.

"The footage looks great. We can wrap up filming the construction next week. We'll do a final reveal the week after." He turned to Irene. "You'll finally have your house back. Thank you so much for putting up with all the chaos that we've created."

"Not at all. It's been enormous fun."

"I know that's not true," Marty said. "You've been most gracious."

"Now that we're almost done, it seems like this project has flown by," Pam said. "How do you like your new bathroom? Is there anything you'd like us to change?"

"Are you kidding? It's so much grander than anything I would have picked out for myself. I'm so grateful to you," she said, grasping Pam's hands in her own and squeezing them. "I've already written to Jed to thank him."

"I'm glad you're pleased, Mom. This project was like a freight train. Once it got rolling, there was no stopping it."

"Jed is extremely pleased with the work you've done," Marty said, "and with the effect the show has had on their business."

"I knew the ratings were good," Steve said. "I'm glad they've translated into revenue for Duncan's."

"Jed's working on another project for the second season," Marty said.

"Really?" Pam clapped her hands together. "That's fantastic. What's he got in mind? Maybe a kitchen remodel?"

"He was thinking of a larger-scale project. Something with a civic component," Marty replied.

"What would that be?" Steve asked.

"He hasn't decided yet. He wants to showcase something that will benefit the community."

"I was in Duncan's yesterday, picking up lightbulbs," Irene interjected. "He had a big sign by the registers, announcing a contest to designate the project for season two of *Wishes of Home*. It said that Duncan's wants suggestions that will make Linden Falls an even better place to live. If they pick your entry, you'll get to name the project."

"It's a genius idea," Marty replied. "Anyone who isn't watching season one will be sure to tune in to season two." He looked from Pam to Steve. "The other thing that will keep viewers watching is the two of you. What do you say—are you up for co-hosting season two?"

"I will—but only if Steve's part of it."

"I'm in," Steve said.

"Great," Marty replied. "I'll text Jed. He's been worried

you might say no. I was, too—until this week. Now that you've made up, you're even better together. That's why we finished filming so quickly tonight. Everything flowed seamlessly."

"Wait—how did you know that we'd…" Steve paused, searching for words, "had a disagreement?"

Marty whipped his glasses off his nose. "Seriously. You think we couldn't tell? Everyone knew. You kept it together when we were filming—like a couple of pros— but the temperature dropped between the two of you the minute I said 'cut.' "

Pam raised her eyes to Steve, and a Cheshire Cat grin sprang onto her lips.

Steve held up one hand. "I know. You don't have to say anything more. Your coffee will be waiting for you in our break room."

Irene and Marty shot each other a puzzled glance.

"Inside joke," Pam said. She took Steve's elbow and hugged it to her side. "Call you tomorrow, Mom," she said. "We're going to get out of here."

The couple strolled away, arm in arm.

CHAPTER 27

"*Y*ou're sure she'll be here?" Pam asked Steve as they arrived at the soccer fields that Saturday at four-thirty.

"Her brother never misses soccer, and she always comes with her mom." He unclipped Chance's harness from the seatbelt in the back seat. Chance jumped to the pavement.

"I don't think he likes riding in the back seat," Pam said. "He's unhappy when I'm in the car."

Chance came up to Pam, wagging his tail.

"He loves you, see? I'm sure he doesn't mind."

"It's safer for you in the back seat," she cooed. "You should ride there all the time—whether or not I'm in the front seat."

Chance continued to stir the breeze with his tail.

"I want Laura to see Chance. I'm sure he's the dog she's been grieving about."

"I think you're right. I can't believe I didn't put two

and two together when you first learned her name. It's such a common surname, it never occurred to me."

"The important thing is that he's here with us now, and she's about to learn that part of her wish on the Wishing Tree came true."

"That tree—again."

"After what happened for us—and now, Chance? Tell me you believe in it." Pam turned earnest eyes to him.

"When you put it like that, I do wonder."

Their conversation was interrupted as Laura Thompson bounded to them across the parking lot.

"That's him!" she screamed. Laura stopped short in front of Chance. She inspected his face, then pointed to his white eyebrow as tears ran down her cheeks and splashed onto the top of his head. She fell to her knees and threw her arms around the dog.

Chance stood, bracing himself against the weight of her with his back legs. He leaned into her, steadying her as sobs wracked her body.

"Where'd you find him?"

"I went to Friends for Life," Pam said, "to get a dog for Steve for his birthday. Chance was still there. I remember how you described him in your wish. I asked the staff about Chance and they told me about… the plans for him… but he was too nice. They had to give him more time to find his forever home."

Laura turned her tear-stained face to Steve. "Will you be good to him?"

"I will," he replied seriously. "He'll have a loving home with me."

She continued to look at Steve, then nodded slowly, as

if agreeing with his statement. "Will you bring him with you on Saturdays so I can see him?"

"Sure."

A carload of fifth graders got dropped off at the entrance. The kids raced by them on their way to the fields, pausing to love up Chance.

"I think coming here will soon be his favorite thing to do."

"The Wishing Tree worked!" Laura sprang to her feet and hugged herself. "Well, it worked for Chance—but only for half of my wish. That's okay, though. I wrote a new one for the other half and hung it on the tree this morning." She looked at Pam. "You believe the tree works, don't you?"

"Of course I do," Pam said. "What did you wish for this time?"

"I entered a contest at Duncan's Hardware this morning when my mom was there buying a new bathroom faucet. I wished that I'd win."

"We heard about that contest—the one for next season's project for *Wishes of Home*?" Pam cast a nervous glance at Steve.

"Yep."

"Great." Pam kept her smile firmly in place.

"The next season's project for *Wishes of Home* is going to be a no-kill animal shelter for Linden Falls. That's how we're going to afford it—Duncan's gives the money." Her head jerked back. "And both of you are going to be the hosts."

Pam and Steve looked at each other, then they both grinned. With the backing of the very determined Laura

Thompson—and the magic of the Wishing Tree—the identity of their new project was a sure thing.

The End

EPILOGUE

*P*am Olson came to a screeching halt outside the Stitchin' Post. She normally power-walked past the large display window of Linden Falls's popular knitting shop. She'd never gotten the hang of either knitting or crochet—no matter how many times her grandmother had tried to teach her when Pam was young. Now that her grandmother was gone, she wished she'd learned.

She sidled over to the window to examine the large throw on display. The chevron pattern was created in five rows of repeating colors ranging from off-white to a rich burgundy brown. The handwritten sign tied to a corner of the throw said that the pattern was known as "Mocha Medley" and promised that it would be an easy project for the beginning knitter.

She took a step back and continued to study it. The throw was gorgeous and masculine. It would be the perfect Christmas gift for Steve. He could get rid of the ratty old blanket that he kept in his drafty family room.

Wasn't he always commenting that he really should get a new one? Pam loved to do her Christmas shopping early and usually had it completed by October first. She'd been wracking her brain on what to get him. This throw would be ideal.

A large chalkboard propped up in the corner of the display window announced that the Stitchin' Post offered weekly knitting lessons. A new class for beginners was starting the next Wednesday evening at seven. This had to be a sign from the Universe.

Pam pushed open the door to the shop, and a bell tinkled overhead. A woman sitting behind the register, her hands wielding a pair of knitting needles at warp speed, looked up and smiled at Pam. Cheryl Paisley placed them into a basket at her feet.

"How can I help?" Cheryl asked. She rose and walked up to Pam, introducing herself. "This is my shop. I'm glad you came in."

"I'm interested in your knitting lessons—for beginners. I saw the throw in the window and I'd like to make that for my boyfriend for Christmas."

"What a lovely gift."

"Is it really a project for a beginner, and do you think I can finish it by Christmas?"

"Yes—and yes!" Cheryl beamed at Pam. "A throw is a big project, but the yarn is bulky and the needles required are large. I made the one in the window and I used a US size 13 needle. Once you get the hang of the pattern, you'll be sailing along without even looking at your hands."

"Like you were just doing when I came in? My grandmother could work a cable stitch without looking. I never knew how she did it."

"Experience and practice," Cheryl said. "Was she a life-long knitter?"

Pam nodded.

"We have knit-ins here all the time. Joining in would help you stay on track. People drop by with their current knitting project and sit over there." She pointed to a circle of chairs in the back of the shop. "There are several experienced knitters who come and they help the novices if they drop a stitch or have problems. I'm always here to help, too."

"That sounds nice—cozy."

"It is. We knit and visit and have a good time. If you want the real scoop about what's going on around Linden Falls, come to a knit-in."

Pam chuckled. "Really?"

"Ask Calvin over at the *Linden Falls Gazette*. He'll tell you. My knitters knew about the sale of the King building before Calvin found out about it. *And* about the plan to make it into an artist's display space and event venue."

"Is that what they're calling King Artisan Market? I heard people talking about it in Duncan's Hardware."

"Yep. And everyone isn't happy about it, I can tell you that." Cheryl arched one eyebrow and leaned toward Pam. "Vendors at the farmer's market on Saturday mornings are worried about the competition."

"My mom has sold her handmade table linens and aprons at the market for years. She's not worried about it."

"You're Irene's girl? I thought you looked familiar. Why don't you both come to our knit-ins?"

"That's a great idea." Pam pointed at the display

window. "I'll take the materials for that throw, and can you sign me up for the lessons beginning this Wednesday?"

"Sure." Cheryl stepped to the register. "Be sure you come to the knit-ins the week after the balloon glow. You wouldn't believe the mischief people get into during that thing! I think it's the combination of darkness and one too many hot toddies to keep the chill off. We always hear the most outrageous stories after the glow."

"Mom and I will be sure to be there." Pam signed the credit card receipt. "Can I leave the supplies for the throw here until Wednesday?"

"Great idea," Cheryl replied. "You'll love the Linden Falls knitters. We're an interesting group."

Don't miss any books in the Wishing Tree series:

Book 10: Overdue Wishes by Tammy L. Grace
Book 11: A Whole Heap of Wishes by Amanda Prowse
Book 12: Wishes of Home by Barbara Hinske
Book 13: Wishful Witness by Tonya Kappes

WE ALSO INVITE you to join us in our My Book Friends group on Facebook. It's a great place to chat about all things bookish and learn more about our founding authors.

FROM THE AUTHOR

Thank you for reading the twelfth book in THE WISHING TREE SERIES. I had such fun creating this world with my author friends from My Book Friends, and I hope you'll read all the books in the series. They're wonderful stories centered around a special tree in Linden Falls. If you enjoyed this story, I also hope you'll explore more of my work. You can find all my books on Amazon.

If you enjoy women's fiction, you'll want to try my bestselling ROSEMONT SERIES, filled with stories of friendship, family, romance, stately homes, and dogs—with a dash of mystery, thriller, and suspense.

My acclaimed GUIDING EMILY SERIES chronicles the life of a young woman who loses her eyesight on her honeymoon and reclaims her independence with the help of her guide dog, proving that *sometimes the perfect partner has four paws.*

If you enjoy holiday stories, be sure to check out THE CHRISTMAS CLUB (adapted for the Hallmark Channel in 2019), PAWS & PASTRIES and its sequel SWEETS & TREATS. They're Christmas stories of hope, friendship, and family.

If you're a fan of mysteries, look for the novels in my "WHO'S THERE?!" collection.

I hope you'll connect with me on social media. You can find me on Facebook, where I have a page and a special group for my readers, and follow me on Amazon, Goodreads, and BookBub so you'll know when I have a new release or a deal. You can also sign up for my newsletter at this link: https://barbarahinske.com/newsletter/

If you enjoyed this book or any of my other books, I'd be grateful if you took a few minutes to leave a short review on Amazon, BookBub, or Goodreads. Just a few lines would be great. Reviews are the best gift an author can receive. They encourage us when they're good, help us improve our next book when they're not, and help other readers make informed choices when purchasing books. Reviews keep the Amazon algorithms humming and are the most helpful aide in selling books! Thank you.

To post a review on Amazon:

1. Go to the product detail page for Wishes of Home on Amazon.com.
2. Click "Write a customer review" in the Customer Reviews section.
3. Write your review and click Submit.

In gratitude,
Barbara Hinske

ABOUT THE AUTHOR

BARBARA HINSKE recently left the practice of law to pursue her writing career full time. Her novella *The Christmas Club* has been made into a Hallmark Channel Christmas movie of the same name (2019), and she feels like she's living the dream. She is extremely grateful to her readers! She inherited the writing gene from her father, who wrote mysteries when he retired and told her a story every night of her childhood. She and her husband share their own Rosemont with two adorable and spoiled dogs. The historic house keeps her husband busy with repair projects and her happily decorating, entertaining, and gardening. She also spends a lot of time baking and—as a result—dieting.

I'd Love to Hear from You! Connect with Me Online:
Sign up for my newsletter at
BarbaraHinske.com to receive your Free Gift,
plus Inside Scoops and Bedtime Stories.
Search for **Barbara Hinske on YouTube**
for tours inside my own historic home plus tips
and tricks for busy women!
Find photos of fictional Rosemont and Westbury,
adorable dogs, and things related to my books at
Pinterest.com/BarbaraHinske.

Hang out with me on Goodreads at
goodreads.com/Barbara_Hinske
Email me at **bhinske@gmail.com** or find me at

Made in the USA
Middletown, DE
03 October 2022